ROMANCE

ANGELA FOXXE

Copyright ©2016 by Angela Foxxe
All rights reserved.

Get Yourself a FREE Bestselling Paranormal Romance Book!

Join the "**Simply Shifters**" Mailing list today and gain access to an exclusive **FREE** classic Paranormal Shifter Romance book by one of our bestselling authors along with many others more to come. You will also be kept up to date on the best book deals in the future on the hottest new Paranormal Romances. We are the HOME of Paranormal Romance after all!

* Get FREE Shifter Romance Books For Your Kindle & Other Cool giveaways

* Discover Exclusive Deals & Discounts Before Anyone Else!

* Be The FIRST To Know about Hot New Releases From Your Favorite Authors

Click The Link Below To Access Get All This Now!

SimplyShifters.com

Already subscribed? OK, *Turn The Page!*

About This Book

Monique had been hiding away in the Northern Vermont Mountains for the previous seven years. Hiding from her past, from her pain and mostly from herself.

However, all that was to change the day she came across an adorable wolf pup who appeared to have a profound effect on her.

Little did she know, the pup was the son of Alpha Wolf Carver who feared his son had been kidnapped.

Upon discovering that his pup was safe and being cared for by Monique, Carver realized he had the opportunity to ask the young girl for one final, life changing, favor....

This is a paranormal shifter romance featuring a handsome, muscle-bound Alpha male and a cute, curvy heroine. It is full of surprises, intrigue and steamy scenes. Please read only if you are 18+

CHAPTER ONE
CHAPTER TWO
CHAPTER THREE
CHAPTER FOUR
CHAPTER FIVE
CHAPTER SIX
CHAPTER SEVEN
CHAPTER EIGHT
CHAPTER NINE
CHAPTER TEN
CHAPTER ELEVEN
CHAPTER TWELVE
CHAPTER THIRTEEN
CHAPTER FOURTEEN

CHAPTER ONE

Living in the mountains that spent most of the year covered in snow came with dangers. Dangers like the pack of wolves who called that area home. They moved with a fluid grace other animals couldn't hope to match. Seven of the largest and fastest worked together to bring down their prey in rapid, decisive attacks. The other ten circled behind the pack to cut off any chance of escape. They also looked after the cubs, wolves too small to join in the hunt, and vulnerable to other predators. Elk, rabbit, and goats all fell before their flashing teeth. There was no escaping the pack.

Snow fell in sporadic bursts, the wind changed direction almost randomly. The alpha wolf didn't like it. Avalanches were always a problem, but were more common with the massive snow storms that came out of nowhere and could freeze an unprotected wolf in a few minutes. He felt just such a storm was coming. His howl echoed off the hillsides and between the trees. The pack sensed his call, more than heard it, as they were spread out over a mile of territory. It was time to go home.

Every wolf, including his mate, charged for the den. Winter quarters in the mountains weren't easy. In the summer they lodged up on the high ridges, frolicking in the sun, or they crept into town unseen. In the winter though, the only place for them was the den.

An old forgotten mine lay a few miles from the lake. It provided access to a plentiful hunting ground, as well as shelter from the weather, and from hunters. It was also well hidden—a fact the wolves took advantage of. While they were prey to no animal, there were others who hunted them.

Recently, the wolves began hearing the howls of a strange pack echoing off the canyon walls. Trouble was coming, and they didn't want it. A rival pack meant competition for food, mates, and space. The alpha knew the real reason they came, though. It wasn't for their winter quarters, or the lake; they felt the call of his son. The same way the pack had.

His son was special, he couldn't say how, but he just knew in his heart. The little cub's birth had been a dramatic affair, and when he finally squeaked out his first growl, something changed. The wolves felt his presence in their minds.

The den lay just ahead as Carver stood watch on a small bluff overlooking the entrance. There were only eight wolves left to check in. Among them, his wife and son. Sienna was more than capable of looking after Kirk, she was married to him after all. He'd picked her for more than just her scent, and her willingness to stand up to him. Her strength of self was remarkable, as was her rust colored coat. He growled at the thought of holding her down and making her his once again.

The den they claimed was big enough for most of the wolves to pair off and find their own space. Unlike many packs, Carver tried to keep an even balance between men and women. Wolves, after all, were very social, and if he could keep them all happy, then there would be no need for them to sneak off to town when the urges called. They were wolves, so the urges called almost every night.

When Sienna and he first started the pack, it hadn't been easy to maintain. He even had to kill a few of the more aggressive males to make sure they understood. The women could choose who they were with. They weren't to be forced or threatened. Sienna came from a pack where the alpha's control stemmed from his ability to force the females into sexual relationships they didn't want. Carver wanted a pack that loved each other, that fought, hunted, and slept together because of a mutual bond, not because of the promise of reward.

It took several years, and more than a few wolves were killed, maimed, and driven out, but Carver had it. Only one wolf in his pack didn't have a mate, and she chose it. Age crept on her and when she did mate, it was in town, far away from the pack.

Carver accepted that as part of who she was. As long as she came back to the pack, he was fine.

The sun reflected off the hill in a bright display of light and color. The call went out and Carver felt the beginnings of worry creeping up his spine. Sienna and Kirk were unaccounted for.

Something was wrong. He threw his head back and howled into the evening sky. The wind picked his voice up and carried it to the corners of the valley.

Nothing.

The pack was safe, he could go look for his mate without worry. The storm on the horizon loomed and there wouldn't be much time before visibility would be non-existent. The wind shifted suddenly, as it did often in this part of the mountain.

New scents came to his nose. He sniffed the air; they were faint, hidden. He, however, was an exceptional tracker, and had been doing it since he was a cub.

Humans.

He took off like a shot. His paws tore through snow as his massive flanks pushed him to run faster than he ever had before. Sienna's scent drifted on the wind, as did Kirk's, but they were off, not quite their scent, they smelled...

Oh gods Sienna, why have you shifted?

If she changed, something catastrophic happened. They rarely shifted in the winter, only a dire emergency would even make them consider taking human form. Usually, the pack stayed wolf for most of the year; in the summer, he and others who wanted to go would take human form and head to town.

There were things in the human world that made existence as a wolf easier. The den was more than just a place to sleep, it was their storage and supply hub. Wolves rarely needed medicine, their own abilities healed them from nearly any wound, and they never got sick. They could starve to death though. Carver traded skins to the local taxidermist for cash and used that to buy emergency supplies to stockpile for hard winters, a practice that saved them more than once.

They followed strict rules when in town. No one could know who they were, they couldn't hurt anyone or draw attention to themselves. It wasn't easy; in human form his wolves were charismatic, and—as far as humans were concerned—desirable.

More than one wolf found him or herself outnumbered in a bar when they attracted the wrong mate. He never let Sienna go by herself; if she needed to, she could defend herself, but not without killing someone.

Now though, she fled from something dangerous, minutes from a storm, and she was in human form. *Why?*

His paws clawed for traction as he came to a stop. The wind still brought her scent to his nose—she was close. As were others. He could smell their sweat... and something else. His ears perked, and he heard her.

She came around a tree, her side bloodied, one arm cradling their pup. Blood flowed down her leg from a wound in her stomach.

"Carver," she screamed, "run!" A bullet exploded out of her chest marring her perfect beauty. Her eyes glazed over. And she was gone. Her body fell face first into the snow. A large dart protruded out of her left buttock, barbed with spines to prevent it from being easily removed.

Kirk wailed where he fell next to his mom. Her red hair splayed out around her head. She didn't move. Carver wanted to scream, he wanted to rage, howl, and kill everyone he could find. He couldn't though. This was no accident. They were looking for him. Kirk yelped as he picked him up by the scruff. There was no time to be gentle. Carver didn't look back as he galloped away from the love of his live. He couldn't cry as a wolf. No matter how much he wanted to.

The den was in sight, he could smell the other wolves fear and anxiety. They were crowded around the entrance, waiting. He wanted to warn them, to tell them to get back. With Kirk in his mouth he couldn't. Fifty feet from the entrance, pain shot up his side. He stumbled in the snow to tumble end over end. Kirk flew from his mouth. He heard the pup's squeak as it bounced off a tree.

Agony, like his leg was on fire, sprang up. He tried to take his feet again, but he couldn't. His paws wouldn't respond, he flopped around in the snow as the pain consumed him. It wasn't a new pain, it was the pain he felt every time he changed. He howled in pain and it finished as the scream of a man. Naked, and in the snow, Carver could barely move. His hand found the barb in his thigh and he tried to pull it free.

When he touched it, he felt the needle end scrape bone. The world went dark from the pain.

The wind picked up, snow started falling and soon the storm would be upon them. He couldn't let them have his pack, no matter the cost. Carver wasn't stupid, he knew the day could come that hunters of some kind would chase them here, or track them.

Feeling returned to his arms and he dragged himself forward. *Twenty feet old man, you can make twenty feet.* He desperately tried to ignore the whine of his pup, he couldn't spare the look now. Whatever they shot him full of prevented his wounds from healing. His face hit the snow and the cold begged him to give up. A warm, rough tongue licked his temple. Despite the situation, Carver smiled; his boy tried to help him.

Footsteps crunched in the hard snow, they weren't far behind. *Just a few more feet. Push!*

He found a fallen tree branch with his hand and heaved. The white bark of the birch tree was no different than the dozen around it. On the trunk of this one, on the south side Carver leaned against, a heart was carved into it. Inside the heart Carver and Sienna had left their initials. They were together when they found the den years before, he only wished they could be together in the end.

"Hang on pup, I love you," he said to his son. The pup whined from the cold. The snow fell faster now. Unless the humans used thermal vision, they wouldn't see the den, or what he held that was buried beneath the trunk of the birch tree.

A form came out of the snow. Covered in tactical garb and a large hat, he held a silenced rifle pointed right at Carver's head.

"You should have stayed in your hole, old man. Now your pack is mine, as is your boy." He dimly recognized the voice, but he couldn't place it.

"Why?" Carver managed to utter. Never in all his long life had a wolf pack attacked another as humans, with guns instead of fangs. No matter the circumstances of his death, the pack would never follow this wolf, not ever. They would fight to the death before they followed a coward.

The man tore off his ski mask to reveal a scarred face. His left eye socket hung empty and claw marks ran down his cheek to his jaw.

Carver's eyes widened in shock. "Brennan?"

The man smiled, he shouldered his rifle a finger brushing against the trigger to activate the laser sight.

"Why are you smiling?" he demanded of Carver.

"You lose." Carver held up the detonator in his hand and thumbed the plunger. It was Brennan's turn for wide-eyed shock. The explosions rippled above them like fireworks. The thunder that followed was the sound of countless tons of snow and rock rushing down the mountain side in a deadly race to the bottom.

Brennan turned to run. Carver hugged his son for the seven seconds he had before the wall of snow crashed into the valley.

*

The radio blared out its usual warnings of winter storms and avalanches as the dark-skinned woman mindlessly chopped logs into firewood. Piece after piece until a thin coat of sweat covered her skin and made her remove her parka. Monique tossed it out of the way. The cold air froze the sweat that made her tank top cling to her generous curves. It refreshed her as she commenced with the wood cutting.

The cabin's wood stores ran low, thanks to an extremely cold winter that didn't seem to want to let go. For the last six years, she lived there. She only needed three cords of wood to make it from October to March. Here it is December and she was down to almost a third of her wood stores.

When the storm let up that morning, she decided it was as good a time as any to add some wood. The flurries of snow billowed about her as she set to work. Piece after piece fell before her axe. It was easy for her, to lose herself in the manual labor. It was why she was there. The howl of a wolf drifted up the valley to her ears. It made her pause. The local pack wasn't usually this active in the winter, and almost always gone in the summer, but that was the second howl she heard today. If they were hunting, they could be dangerous.

That's enough wood for today.

She carried the axe back to the small shed behind the cabin. It only took her a moment to clean it off and oil the blade to help it fight off the damp snow. The last thing she needed was a rusty wood axe. The snow picked up in the few minutes it took her to put her tools away and stack the wood she chopped under the cabin's south awning. She reached down to pick up her coat when she heard the terrible noise that no mountain person ever wanted to hear.

Avalanche!

The ferocity of the rumble shook the ground. She stumbled to the side of the cabin to hold on. It was worse than any earthquake she ever felt. Across the valley, nearly a mile away, she watched as the entire side of the mountain gave way and rolled at breakneck speed into the valley. The snow obscured the results, but she prayed no one was caught in it.

No, don't think about it. Don't think about it!

Tears threatened her. Monique wiped her face and refused to give in. The rumbling quieted as the danger passed.

Inside her cabin once more, she stripped down out of her wet clothes. In the cold, wearing wet undergarments meant death. She put a few more logs on the fire to build it up. A line ran in front of it that she used to dry her clothes. Clad in a fresh pair of white panties that contrasted against her dark skin, and a sports bra to hold her generous curves in place, Monique started in on her pastime. There wasn't much to do up in the mountains. She hunted in the summer, and when she couldn't kill enough food, she traded with the people of Albury, the small town twenty miles away and three thousand feet down the mountain.

"One," Monique said to the air as she completed her first push-up. For the next hour, she worked her upper body with a variety of push-ups, pull-ups, and other resistance training. When she first moved there, she only wanted to escape New Orleans. Her body wasn't ready for the rigor of surviving in the mountains, though. After the first winter when she nearly froze to death because she couldn't chop down a tree, she resolved to get in better shape. After digging through the chest her uncle left behind she found an army manual for physical fitness. The workouts honed her muscles and kept her mind from turning to darker thoughts.

After she finished that, Monique set to making sure her bow was in good working order. Ammo was too expensive and, with the avalanche danger, she didn't want to risk firing a rifle. The bow she bought with what little money remained after she left New Orleans. The arrows she learned to craft herself, along with how to hunt with it.

The wind whipped the fire into a frenzy; she could hear the gale howling outside. She put her bow aside and started in on dinner. This was her routine, day in, and day out. Her fingers and thoughts always focused on survival, always on what to do next. Never looking back. She left that for her nightmares.

CHAPTER TWO

The cabin didn't have electricity, which meant Monique went to bed when the sun went down, and rose when it came up. It took her some time to get used to it, but after a few months, she slept better than she had her whole life. If it weren't for her nightmares, she could imagine looking forward to sleep. She woke with a start, clutching her throat and gasping for air, just like every morning since... *No, no, no.*

It was her ritual. She sprang naked out of bed to run to the fire. Its embers ran low, but not dead. Dried leaves, grass, and twigs brought it back to life. When the flames looked ready, she gingerly placed a small amount of wood to stoke them. After a few minutes, a full sized log roared and crackled. The warmth of the stove warded off the cold, and dried the sweat that covered her dark skin.

Once the cabin warmed a few degrees, she tested the water—it wasn't frozen. She could take a three minute shower every few days and have enough water to last the winter. Today was a shower day. Monique's skin tone was a gift from her African father, a rich brown color that stretched from head to toe. Not overly black, nor obviously white, but certainly dark. Her hair and eyes came from her mother. Silky black hair fell in long, straight waves past her shoulders. Combined with her green eyes, it made her unusual enough to stand out.

In New Orleans, as a child, the children called her white chocolate, and not as a term of endearment.

The irony in a city with a predominately black people, and a rich French history, people being racist to her immigrant French mother and African father wasn't lost to her.

She shook the memory of her past lest it lead to places she didn't want to go. The clock counted down, she had less than two minutes to finish. The straight razor smoothed her legs and pubis over. She couldn't afford any hair for a tick to get lost in, plus she liked the feel of her smooth skin. With twenty seconds left, she let the water hit her shoulders and flow down her back. The timer dinged and the water shut off.

A quick look out the window was enough to tell her what she needed to wear. Her black, cold weather boots, wool pants, a thin tank top, and her jacket over that. The jacket was rated for below zero.

In anything more than twenty degrees, she kept it unzipped to keep her cool. The thermometer stayed level at thirty since she got up. It wouldn't be getting much warmer, and probably not colder until the sun started its trek downward.

The fresh snow made it easy to track. With winter being harsher than normal, she decided adding a couple of rabbits to her stores would be wise. For now, the storm abated and Monique needed to get to work.

She put another log on the fire and adjusted her mental math on how long it would last. She hated trying to restart it, and if she were freezing, she may not be able to. Best to let it stay aflame than risk having to start a new one.

Living up in the mountains for the past several years gave Monique an almost sixth sense when it came to her area. When she stepped out into the fresh snow, she felt a tingle up her spine. Something wasn't right. Her bow came up with an arrow knocked in a heartbeat.

"Whoa there lady!" The voice came from her left. Monique dropped to her knee, and lined up her arrow with the chest of the man who spoke.

"Hey, I said hold it, don't make me say it again." The man who spoke was on the road atop a horse, his beige parka bore the insignia of sheriff. It took her a second to recognize him. When she first moved here, she spent a lot of time in town. The cabin needed a lot of work. Now though, she only went once toward the end of summer. *What was his name... Petrov?* He was a Russian immigrant, and when she was last in town, he had only been a deputy. Every time she went though, he found some reason to talk to her. His come-ons were obnoxious, and she always got the feeling he looked down on her because of her heritage. Not a lot of black people lived in Russia.

She let the string slacken and lowered the bow, but not by much.

"You're on my land without permission, Deputy, is there a reason?" She couldn't remember the last time she spoke aloud. Her French accent came out thick for lack of practice.

"It's Sheriff now, Monique, and I would think you would be a little more hospitable to a man looking for a lost baby." His smile told her all she needed. He was scum, and he couldn't be trusted.

"Good luck with that. Now get off my land."

His smile went flat. "How about a cup of coffee? It's damn cold up here."

Monique didn't budge. As far as she was concerned, this conversation was over.

"You're an awful stubborn *girl.* Stuck up here on your own, refusing kind gestures, what happens if you get hurt, or you need something? You would be smart to remember that."

She didn't mind being called a girl, after all, she was one, but the way he said it was an insult. Her eyes narrowed and her fingers flexed around the bowstring.

"*Sheriff*, I want to be left alone, do you understand that? Leave; I won't ask again." There was menace in her voice as she spoke, and something else. The pain of being around people was too much. Too many memories came back and wanted to overwhelm her. It was easier to just focus on surviving.

He growled at her, spun his horse around, and kicked it in the flanks. The horse took off at a trot. Monique lifted an eyebrow at the growl. *I'm going to need to improvise some locks on my door. Sharpen my knife, and make sure the pistol is loaded tonight.*

Men like him were trouble. They had egos a mile long, and when that ego was hurt, they would lash out physically. Monique was well aware of the dangers of such men, and wouldn't allow herself to fall victim.

She waited until she couldn't hear the horse anymore and then set out in the opposite direction.

Fifteen minutes passed since she exited the cabin, and that was less time she could use for hunting.

The fresh snow held plentiful tracks, several hare, a fox hunting, like her, she even came across a deer. It wasn't unusual for the winter, but she wouldn't hunt deer in the snow. She only needed three or four in a year, and she always chose them in the fall, after the fawns grew enough to take care of themselves.

An hour into her expedition, with a little over half again as much time left, Monique came across wide deep tracks that looked like paws.

Wolves...

Three of them. Big ones from the looks of the tracks. *That's odd...* The deer and wolf tracks intersected, but the wolves didn't turn to track it. The wind swept down from the ridge-line at her back toward the valley, as long as she kept the wolves upwind of her, they would likely leave her alone. They would only attack a person to defend cubs or if they were extremely hungry. The food on the mountain was plentiful enough that she figured they would leave her be.

She picked a path that would keep the wolves above her, but didn't follow the deer tracks on the off chance the wolves were hunting it. A hundred yards later, she found the rabbit tracks she was looking for. With a nocked arrow, and slow movements, she came across the snow bunny. It nibbled on a plant that somehow escaped the snowfall of the night before. She lifted the arrow to her eye, and placed the rabbit right below the arrow head. Slowly, enough that her breath barely steamed, she let it out. Halfway through, the arrow flew.

The second she released, she ran after it. The arrow hit the rabbit in the haunches and spun it over several times. She fell on the little creature with her knife and finished the job. She wasn't cruel enough to let the animal suffer. A whimper from behind set her in motion. She rolled on one shoulder and came up with her bow nocked.

"Shit," she said to the baby wolf. It couldn't have been more than a few months old. He limped out from the tree that provided shelter. The little wolf found the dropped rabbit. His tongue came out to lick the blood off the fur.

"Well little guy, I think that's your family I came across; they must be looking for you." Wolf cubs were dangerous, she knew that. Come between a mom and her baby, the instinct was natural... Monique closed her eyes, her hands flexed into tight, trembling fists. *Breathe girl, breathe.* When she opened her eyes, the wolf pup limped over to her boot, his right forepaw held up to avoid putting pressure on it. Monique could see the bone sticking out.

"Oh pup, you're dead, aren't you? Your family can't fix that." The little pup whimpered again at her. *What are you doing? Leave him the rabbit and walk away.*

Almost as if he could hear her thoughts, he whimpered again.

No. Walk away.

With a breath for resolve, she turned and walked. The little pup whined after her. His little voice pierced the iron coat she wore around her heart.

*

Carver gasped for air. Cold penetrated him, froze him. He couldn't feel his extremities, and everything was black. *Where am I? Oh god, the avalanche! Kirk!*

He called the wolf, if he could shift he would be out of the snow.

Nothing.

Damn Brennan, what have you done?

Anger flooded his system. He couldn't shift, and he didn't know why, but he didn't need to be the wolf to be strong. He howled as he pushed against his icy coffin with all his might. The sight of his beloved crashing to the snow dead fuelled his rage. The loss of his son in the avalanche, the betrayal by one he once called friend, all of it. His heart pounded and he thought his chest would explode. His arm moved an inch, then a little more. Light pierced the snow and his hand was free. It took only moments from there to free his whole body.

Carver rested against the top of the tree and breathed easy. The barbed dart still stuck out of his thigh. His struggle to get free tore his wound open sending fresh blood to drop on the snow. The barbs were such that if he tried to remove it, he would lose a half pound of flesh easy, and he couldn't bandage it, since any movement would just start the bleeding again. He needed to get help. The entrance to the mine was buried under twenty feet of snow and rock. The avalanche changed the way everything looked, he couldn't even tell where it was. The emergency exit was on the other side of the mountain. Even healthy and in good weather it would take him two days to reach it.

Carver collapsed against the tree. His struggle to not die in the snow was for naught. He would die above it. His love and son would go un-avenged. Carver took a deep breath to calm his heart when he caught a familiar scent.

"No... It's not—" he didn't want to say it. Didn't want to hope it could be true. He struggled to stand and the wound in his thigh burned with each movement. His legs didn't want to work at first. He struggled with each foot fall. On the third step they loosened, by the tenth he only walked with a limp. Thirty feet from where he started he fell to his knees. A small tunnel in the snow, just big enough for a pup, protruded here. He bent down to smell. *Kirk, you're alive boy. Alive!* Now he had something to fight for. The pup was hurt, that much was obvious. He headed off to the west, up the mountain.

"Good boy, let them climb to try and find you." Carver wasn't helpless as a human, but it wasn't his natural form, it wasn't where he shined. He stumbled up the hill, each step a clumsy attempt to not fall and hurt his leg even more. Kirk's scent drifted left and right, but always came back to the center. It wasn't an easy climb, not even if he could have shifted. When his foot slipped and he fell to his knee, the barbed dart spurted blood. Only his remarkable regeneration kept him from dying out of blood loss. It wasn't infallible though, he would need to eat soon or he would die.

His heart jumped when he found the wolf tracks; they were hunting him. The line of their tracks however, ran off in the wrong direction. *They don't know what he smells like. They're hunting everything, running down everything. That will take time.*

After what felt like weeks of climbing, he made it to the top of the ridge line. He accepted that he was easy to follow, leaving a trail of blood and sweat behind. It would only be a matter of time before they found him. He needed to find Kirk first.

The fresh scent of a kill perked him up. His mouth watered and his heart sped up. Had his son managed to kill a rabbit? He smiled at the thought. Kirk was too new, though, too young. His teeth were barely formed.

He found the rabbit's blood against a tree, tiny bits of discarded flesh that smelled like Kirk had nibbled on them. What he saw next sent fear to his heart. Boot prints in the snow. He knelt down beside them placing his fingers inside the print. The snow was hard on the edges, that meant it had time to re-freeze, the human was at least an hour ahead of him.

Whoever it was wasn't trying to hide their tracks, but they were carefully, and cleverly keeping their scent downwind from the other wolves. Carver smiled. That meant they were upwind from him. He caught Kirk's scent, it mingled with another scent. His pupils dilated and his skin heated. *Woman,* his mind told him. The hunter that held his son took off to the north. He followed.

It was slow going with the barb in his thigh, but at least the hill was much easier on top of the ridge than at the bottom. His pack hunted south, where the valley and the river connected. Rarely did they follow the deer up the mountain. Too many calories were lost climbing for a meal that may not happen. Now he had no choice. Whoever was up here wasn't an amateur. The path she picked to follow kept the wolves away from her scent while offering her an easy walk to wherever she was going.

He caught a whiff of wood smoke. A cabin couldn't be far away. What would he do though? It's not like he could barge in and demand his son. The human wouldn't even know what he was talking about. And he wasn't in a position to fight. All his instincts told him to run in and save his son. He fought to suppress them. Whoever had the boy wasn't going to hurt him. The boot prints were the only prints, yet he smelled Kirk, which meant they carried him. He had time to figure out a plan, he just had to find them first. And hope the others didn't.

CHAPTER THREE

The little pup squeaked as Monique examined his leg. She wasn't a doctor, and certainly not a vet, but she knew enough to see signs of infection.

"This must have just happened, no?" The pup's pant made her smile. She had him on her kitchen table. When she got home, she placed him there along with some very small slices of meat and a little bowl of water. He couldn't move well on his own, and she couldn't honestly imagine how he got so far without help. But he did. The rabbit needed to be skinned though, and it couldn't wait.

The pup lay on the table patiently as she went to work with her skinning knife. She tore the skin from the rabbit by cutting it at the hind quarters, then pulling it down to its headless neck. The rabbit she hung over a bowl to make sure the blood was drained, the skin she put in a sink full of cold water.

Every few seconds she glanced up, the pup's ears would perk up and he nibbled on some meat, or lapped up the water. Monique smiled, a genuine one. *Oh god, stop. Just stop. You can't keep him, you don't want this.*

She redoubled her efforts to focus on flaying the rabbit. Once she had the chunks of meat in the sizes she wanted, they all went into freezer bags and then out the little hole in the back of the cabin she used as her cold storage.

When she returned to him, the food and water were gone. Carefully, so not to aggravate his paw, she examined him again. He panted happily at her, his pink tongue darted out to lick her fingers.

"Stop it," she said with a force she didn't mean. He whined at her. Then tried to lick her fingers again. "Dammit pup, stop it." She didn't want to smile, didn't want to feel anything. Certainly not for a pup that would likely die on her.

"Wait a second," she murmured. Did she have the wrong paw? She turned the leg over and ran her fingers through the short fur. The break was gone. Not healed, not hidden, gone. Like it never was there. Had she imagined it?

No, not possible. I saw the bone, the blood. He broke his leg.

The pup's ears shot up and he growled. It came out as more of a high pitched whine than an actual growl, but it was enough that Monique knew something was wrong. She scooped the pup up and placed him in the corner, wrapped in a towel.

"Stay here little guy, out of sight. If it's your parents out there, we need to wash you off before we give you back to them."

Monique checked the clock, almost five meant the sun would be going down soon. The way the dark clouds gathered on the horizon it was a sure bet a storm brewed. *Great, another one.* This winter was already the coldest one since she moved up here, and long, too. If it went on too much longer, she would have to make the hike down to the ranger station and get the four-wheeler. Town was a long way away on foot. At least with the ATV she could be there and back in a day. Some things she needed she couldn't make herself or hunt.

The wind picked up outside sending snow against the big window that dominated the front wall. It held a view of the slope, letting her see for a half mile down to the tree line. A figure appeared out of the snow. It was the sheriff.

"Great, pup, not your parents." The aggravation in her voice rang in the pup's growl. "I know, he's a tool, and possibly dangerous, but so am I." The third drawer down next to the table held her pistol. A vintage WWII .45 automatic her great uncle carried. He cared for it like a child, and Monique did, too. She pulled the slide back, clicked the safety on to hold it in place, then slid it in the small of her back. Her nylon belt held it snugly. She pulled her tank top down to cover it.

She opened the door just as he knocked.

"I thought I told you to get off my land?"

A dark shadow fell over his face. He didn't look happy. "I lost my horse to some wolves. I need to use your radio." He tried to step forward but Monique didn't budge.

"You can't make it to the ranger station? It's only seven miles."

"You're seriously not going to let me use your radio? I could die if this storm hits." The look of exasperation on his face sent her nerves on fire. What she wanted to do was punch him in his stupid head. But he was right, she couldn't let him die. As much as she wanted to be left alone...

"All right, fine, but you'd better make it quick." She moved aside. He nodded and walked into the cabin. Her place wasn't particularly big. Monique maintained the place in an orderly fashion—no dirty dishes, or old food, her clothes were put away, and her sleeping bag lay rolled up at the foot of the very small bed. From the fireplace on the back wall to the front door was only twenty feet, and thirty feet from the bed to the kitchen.

He pointed to the radio questioningly.

"Yeah, that's it."

"It's old isn't it?"

"It came with the place."

She suddenly felt very out of place in here own cabin, and she didn't like it. The bed offered her some comfort letting her put her back to the wall and watch his every move. She suddenly wished she put a real top on, and not one that showed cleavage. He kept looking at her from the side, in an obvious attempt to check out her boobs without checking them out.

"It must get lonely up here. I never see you in town anymore. How come?"

She gritted her teeth. "I like to be alone."

He nodded and smiled. "I can understand that." His eyes passed over the towel that hid the pup. *That's the second time he's looked at it.*

"Have you heard or found anything today? Anything at all could be useful to us." That feeling of things being wrong spiked in her gut. What was he doing?

"Aren't you going to call your friends for help?"

He chuckled. "That's exactly what I'm going to do." His voice took on a thick tone. In a flash, he pulled his jacket off and unbuttoned his shirt leaving him bare-chested. The pup growled from the corner.

"You should have left him in the woods Monique. There was no reason for you to get involved in this. I had plans for a tasty morsel like you."

She didn't know why the man wanted the pup, or why he took his shirt off and looked at her like she was his next meal, and she didn't care. She pulled the .45 out and squeezed the trigger in one swift motion. It would be easier to explain his death than hers. The pistol's earth shattering roar filled the cabin as she squeezed off three rounds into his center mass. Petrov rocked back against the counter. Not down, he tore the radio off the wall and threw it at her.

She hadn't expected him to live after the first round, let alone three. The radio slammed into her shoulder. She grunted as she fell backwards on the bed. Before her back touched the bed, he was there. Hands pinned her wrists down so tight her fingers went numb and the pistol fell out. His bloody torso was inches from her. She watched in horror as the wounds healed, the bullets fell out with a clink. In seconds, it was like he never was hurt.

"Now," he said in his strange voice, "I'm going to fuck you till you beg me to stop, then I'm going to eat you alive. You should have given me that cup of coffee."

She spat in his face. His lips curled up in anger. His next word was lost in a snarl. He looked down to shake the pup off his leg. The poor thing flew across the cabin with a squeak. He put both her wrists in one hand and held them above her head.

Monique squirmed under him, but his grip was like a vice. She couldn't get any traction, and he weighed far more than he looked. When she tried to buck him off, he just laughed.

"Struggle all you want. I like fighters, they're all the more sweet a conquest." His free hand ripped her shirt and bra off, the straps cut into her painfully before snapping.

"No!" she screamed. "No!"

His hand fell on her large breasts, his laugh filled her ears. He leaned down to kiss her neck. The door banged open form the wind and he ignored it. His fingers pulled on her tits and he tried to force his mouth over hers.

Large hands wrapped around his neck and pulled him backward off of her. She jumped up the second she was free. Someone, she couldn't see who, held him around his neck and under one arm, with his legs around his torso. They both growled and screamed obscenities as they struggled.

Fuck this. Her pistol wasn't hard to find, she put a boot in his torso and stuck the pistol to his temple.

"No wait," he screamed.

"Burn in hell." The gun roared, splattering his brains over the tile floor.

*

Carver didn't move. He lay on the floor holding the remains of Petrov's body. She didn't just fire once, she pulled the trigger until the slide locked back. Intentional or not, she killed a wolf. He sighed inwardly, *The poor human, she doesn't know the world she's stepped into.* Once his pack found out, they would never let her live, regardless of the circumstances. She stood above him breathing heavily. Her eyes looked trapped. Carver's eyes were on hers, as tempting as her body was to look at, he didn't want her to think he was another would-be-rapist.

She certainly was a world of difference than the natives of Vermont, or the tourists even. Her skin, while not black, had a smooth satiny look to it and was far darker than Carver's. She was fit, for sure, he could make out the hints of muscle in her abs, something that was particularly difficult for women. The thing he was most drawn to, though, were her sea green eyes. Carver had never seen the ocean, but he imagined it was the same color as her eyes.

She wasn't moving to cover herself, almost as if she expected to wake up. Carver carefully pushed the remains of the other wolf off of him. He held his hands out in front of him.

"It's okay, I'm not here to hurt you." He said each word with care. It snapped her eyes back to the present. She looked down at the gun, the slide locked open, the chamber empty. Then back at him. He could see she was in shock. He remembered well the first time he was forced to kill a human. It wasn't a memory he cherished.

"My name's Carver, I'm going to get up now, okay?" He moved his hands to help him stand.

Startled she took a step back. He got to his knees and went no higher.

"What's your name?" He could see her eyes clearing, control coming back over her face. Her cheeks flared red and her smell completely changed. She was going to be okay.

"Close the door before we freeze to death," she muttered. He moved to the door slowly. He kept his back to her, trusting that she wasn't reloading. When he heard the sound of fabric on skin he knew she trusted him, at least a little. He secured the door shut. His entrance ruined the pitiful lock that normally held it closed, so he jammed a bit of wood to keep it shut amidst the wind that picked up with every second.

Outside the window, the visibility dropped to almost nothing. He could feel the pressure changing and the storm coming. It was going to be big. He felt something rub against his leg.

"Kirk," he whispered. He dropped to his knees and hugged his son to his chest. He couldn't hold back the tears. His little pup licked his face and made squeaking noises.

"I thought he was a wolf pup, but I guess he's your dog?" Carver bristled at the unintended slight.

"He is mine," he said through clenched teeth. "And I thank you for caring for him. I thought I would never see him again." The pup yipped at him, not a bark, but more of a high pitched cough. The dark-skinned woman smiled at that.

"I didn't get your name," he said politely, scratching Kirk's ears. There wasn't a scratch on him. *How did he survive the avalanche and not get hurt?*

"Monique, uh, yeah, just Monique." Carver smiled, her voice sounded soft and sweet. It hid a lot of pain though. He could understand that.

"Thank you for helping me with... with... this," she finally said lamely. "Whatever this is."

"I'm sorry for what he tried to do. I hope you understand we're not all like that." He didn't know how much she knew already, and he didn't want to be the one to fill in the blanks for her.

"Right, not all men are rapists, just the ones I meet." He cocked an eyebrow up and started to speak when she continued, "Why are you naked?"

He forgot that he wore nothing. The wolf couldn't come as long as the barb in his leg injected its poison into his system. Finding Kirk seemed far more important than clothes. If he was going to stay human though, he would need protection.

"I was in an avalanche, it's when I lost Kirk." He suppressed the memory of Sienna, he couldn't grieve for her now, though he wanted to. He wanted to fall to his knees and scream her name, but he couldn't.

"I must have lost my clothes then." The cabin wasn't huge, and the smell of the dead body already filled the air. *We can't stay here.*

"I'm really sorry, Monique, but we have to go." She looked blankly at him, then the door.

"You want to go out in a snowstorm naked?"

He opened his mouth to speak, but she was right, he needed clothes. Petrov's discarded shirt and jacket would help, but his pants weren't fit to be worn, and his feet were too small.

"I don't suppose you have any men's boots around?"

He pulled on the shirt and jacket, feeling awkward standing in her kitchen, naked from the waist down. To her credit, she didn't look at him. But that would change, it was why he needed to go. He couldn't be around her for much longer before his hormones kicked in.

She dug through an old Army foot locker in the corner; it looked vintage to him. She came out with a pair of boots and pants that looked like they might fit. It was unusual for him to find clothes that fit, simply because he was bulky. Six feet tall and two hundred pounds of muscle made it hard to find pants to wear. Apparently though, the man who wore these previously was of similar stature.

"My uncle, well, great uncle, he carried ammo on the beaches of Iwo Jima. That man could lift a car. You have a similar build." She answered the question his face asked. Carver pulled the pants on; they were old, but still in good shape. The boots were a little newer, not much, and they were well worn. It would be enough for him to get to a cave and get this barb out.

He winced as the pants pulled on the dart. Monique noticed.

"What's wrong?"

"I was hurt in the avalanche, nothing to worry about. Thank you for your hospitality, but I really have to go. You're going to want to store that," he pointed at the body, "somewhere air-tight." She nodded.

He scooped up Kirk on his way to the door. The little pup whined at him. "No," he said quietly. If Monique thought it odd he spoke to the wolf, she didn't say anything.

"Well, thanks again for helping him." The door opened easy enough. The wind blustered and snow whipped in every direction. The pup whined some more.

"Yeah, you too." She sounded lost, broken.

You know what they'll do to her. You're leaving her to die. He couldn't help her, he had to focus on Kirk. No one else mattered. He was a dozen steps from the cabin when Kirk started squirming.

"Hold still boy, we can't help her, no one can." The pup didn't agree. He pushed with his hind legs and surged over Carver's shoulders. Carver sighed. The little pup was insistent.

CHAPTER FOUR

Monique stared blankly at the body on the floor. Her mind was slow to respond; she couldn't form thoughts or take action. Everything seemed like it was in molasses around her. The strange naked man who saved her left almost as fast as he arrived. Now there was a body to deal with, a door to fix, and from the sound of it, the storm raged on outside.

She looked down at herself, the white turtle neck she pulled over her head didn't feel like much protection. Not against the elements or anything else. At least Carver turned out to be a decent guy, he didn't try to take advantage of the situation, not like...
No. Full stop. Fix the door, hide the body, survive. Focus.

The little pup suddenly careened through the door, his wet paws slid on the tile as he tried to negotiate a corner. He tumbled over to land in a pile at her feet. Carver came in right behind him.

"I'm sorry, he doesn't want me to leave you and this is his way of telling me."

Uh huh, sure. She started to think twice about him being a "good guy." She looked around for her gun; it lay on the bed where she dropped it. Almost as if he read her mind, Carver lifted his hands in the air.

"Listen, I know this has been a strange day, but Kirk is right. If I leave you here, you'll die." That cleared her mind. Her eyes narrowed as she made her way to the bed. He made no move to stop her.

"That is of limited use, as I'm sure you realize." The vision of Petrov on top of her, the bullets extruding from his flesh to drop on the floor, flashed through her mind. She knelt beside the bed, and sure enough, three .45 slugs lay in little pools of blood on the floor.

"What was he?" She couldn't shake the feeling that her nightmare wasn't over. *I came here to escape this, dammit. It's not fair.*

"I can explain, honestly, but we have to go. They will be drawn to his death and we don't want to be here when they get here."

Monique ran her hands over her face. This was too much. Too much weirdness, and yet something strangely familiar, mixed at once. She looked at the body, the pup in the door with his big yellow eyes looking at her, and Carver. Something about him told her she could trust him. But she made that mistake before.

"Listen, seconds matter, get what you need to survive, but we have to go," he implored her. His tone decided it; he seemed genuinely afraid. Not the typical "trust me baby" she was used to.

"Okay, give me a sec." If they were going out in a storm, she wanted her full kit. The pack lay against the wall almost fully loaded. She stuffed the pistol, the spare box of ammo, and her extra first aid kit. *What am I doing?*

What you always do—survive. In less than five minutes, she stood at the door, ready to go. Carver scooped up the little pup and headed out into the storm. Monique followed along, lowering her goggles so the snow wouldn't blind her. The fresh powder was already an inch thick, and with the weight of her full kit on her back, she had to take each step carefully.

I must be in shock, she realized when she didn't know where they were going. They just left the safety of a cabin to head blindly out into a snowstorm. Monique looked back over her shoulder; even if she turned around, she wasn't certain she could find her way back to the cabin. With no other options for the moment, she trudged forward following the man who saved her.

Over the next hour, the weather only got worse. Blustering snow turned into a full on gale. Even with her parka, she couldn't stay out for long.

"Hey," she yelled to Carver. "Hey, we need shelter." She wasn't sure he heard her until he turned his head and nodded. He pointed off to his left, and started walking that way. Monique followed, the ground turning up hill. *God, that's all I need, go up hill and get exhausted.*

He didn't go far. Monique blinked and he was gone. The snow swirled around her as she took a tentative step where he was. The snow parted to reveal a cave entrance. *Better than freezing to death.*

She pulled a road flare from her pocket, struck it, and tossed it into the cave. Red light illuminated the walls that disappeared deeper in. At the very edge of the light, she made out Carver's form. He waved her forward. She trusted him this far, and he had saved her. Something about him awakened her, made the last seven years fade.

She found him in a small room off the main cave. It was big enough for four people to lay down in, with a little shoot in the roof that sounded like it went to the outside. She picked up her flare and put it in the center of the cave before she sat down.

"There's no wood," Monique realized. She could start a fire, but without a fire source it would do her no good.

"We'll be safe in here, the wind..."

"It's not the wind, it's like five degrees below zero in here. I'm gonna freeze to death without a fire." She was genuinely alarmed, at least when she was moving her own body heat kept her warm along with her parka. Now, though, out of the wind, there was a whole new danger. The only position that presented itself wasn't one she cared for. Her survival instinct kicked in though.

"Take your jacket off," she said. She unzipped her parka and shed it next to her pack. Her body shivered from the sudden cold. In her pack, she dug out her sleeping bag, it was rated for the temperature she expected to encounter, and she never thought she would be stupid enough to go out on the mountain in the winter. With the bag laid out, she stripped down to her underwear and crawled in. She held it open for him. He didn't move.

"In about five minutes this cave is going to be an icebox, if we're not both in here to share body heat, we're both dead."

"You don't understand..."

"Carver, god knows why, but I trusted you, get your ass in here," she growled. He moved. The sleeping bag was big, but it wasn't meant for two. Carver slid in next to her, his hard body gliding down the length of hers sending little lightning bolts into her. Parts of her that hadn't felt anything in years began to wake as if from a long slumber.

"You're warm," she murmured as she tucked her arms into his chest. Monique felt emotions stirring in her she thought long buried. Something about this mysterious man brought out the wounds in her heart.

"Monique, what happened to you, why are you up here?" he asked, as his arms wrapped around her to draw her in tight. The bag was suddenly very warm for her. She could feel her wall coming down.

She wanted to tell him things she didn't want to tell her self, things she hid from these last years.

"I was in a hospital," she heard herself say, not believing that it was she that spoke. "I'd just had a baby. My parents were there with me. The father... well, he didn't stick around."Carver pushed the hair back from her face, the tender gesture sent goose bumps up and down her skin.

"You're cold," he murmured, he brushed his lips against her forehead. Monique let out a long sigh. "Go on," he urged.

"We lived in New Orleans, and there was this big storm. I didn't find out till afterwards what they called it. The hospital evacuated, but somehow I got left behind with my baby." The tears started rolling down her cheeks uncontrollably. "They wheeled us into this waiting area and then left us. I kept waiting for them to come back, then the flood waters came and..." She couldn't hold back the sobs.

"I tried Carver, I tried so hard, I couldn't stop the water from..." He didn't need her to say any more, the sadness in her heart told the story.

"It wasn't your fault, you did everything you could. Sometimes bad things happen and there's nothing we can do about it."

She buried her head in his chest and cried. It felt like hours later her tears dried and the weight that she carried around with her for seven years lifted.

"How... how did you do that?"

"Monique," he whispered, "I'm not what I appear to be. I have gifts, and sometimes they can be used to help bring the truth out."

For her, all she cared about was the terrible guilt that punished her for years, guilt about not saving her baby, about losing her parents, and the terrible ordeal she suffered getting out of New Orleans, it was all gone. She looked up into his brown eyes, and without thinking she kissed him. He froze at her touch, she poured everything she had into that one kiss. He froze at first but soon relented. Her tongue slipped inside of his mouth and they explored each other. She felt him harden next to her. Her whole body vibrated with excitement and emotions she hadn't felt in years.

Kirk whined and covered his little eyes with his paws. They broke the kiss to chuckle at the pup.

"Carver, I don't want to go back to the way things were, please let me feel something good for once, something wonderful."

He kissed her again, nibbling on her lips. His hands explored her back until they found her bra and gracefully unclipped it. She wriggled free of it, exposing her large breasts to him. His kisses trailed down her collarbone to her chest, each one leaving a little trail of fire behind it. He sucked one of her nipples into his mouth, swirling his tongue around it. Monique let out a low moan of pleasure that almost sounded like a purr. Her panties matted to her naked flesh from how wet she was. He rolled her over, shedding the bag, but she didn't feel cold, the whole room was warm and inviting. He stood on his knees to remove his pants. She gasped at his size. In the dark of the cabin, she hadn't noticed but his dick hung down at least ten inches. She took a deep breath as he pulled her panties down. She lifted her hips to let him in.

Carver leaned down to breathe hotly against her pussy. She moaned as the air rolled over her sensitive bits. He ran a finger gently over her lips, up and down. Her hips gyrated at the attention. Her insides were on fire and she could feel her juices flowing down her legs.

His tongue brushed against her sensitive clit and she nearly came. He ran his tongue up her slit and then flicked it against her hood. Large fingers gently pushed inside of her and she thought she would die from the pleasure. With plenty of lubrication, he increased the tempo of his fingers, sawing them in and out of her while he licked the top of her clit, careful not to touch the most sensitive part.

"Oh god, Carver, oh fuck, don't stop." Her hands came down and pushed his head against her body. He added a third finger, while he simultaneously sucked on her clit, pulling it into his mouth and flicking it with his tongue.

That was all she could take, her back arched, one of her hands grabbed her tits and squeezed and she came in one massive explosion that left her seeing red.

"Oh fuck," she screamed as her climax peaked. His mouth sucked her juices and she could hear his throat swallow each wave of her. She couldn't focus on anything, the pleasure she felt came in waves. His hands picked her up and rolled her over, gently he placed her down on her knees. She felt his huge cock slide between her legs. He lifted her up so her back leaned against his front with both of them on their knees. One hand reached round her and squeezed her breasts and played with her nipples. He rolled them in his fingers and gently pulled on them.

Each movement elicited purrs and moans from her. His other hand followed the line of her belly down to her naked sex. He pressed his middle finger into her slit and moved it up and down. She ground her ass into him, rocking her hips forward so her pussy lips slid to either side of his dick.

With a long stroke of his finger, which sent her into dizzying heights of pleasure, he slid his dick forward and pressed the head past her lips.

"Oh, oh, oh god," she moaned. "It wont fit," she murmured. He kissed her neck down to her shoulders and squeezed her nipple with his finger.

"It will," he said between kisses. He pushed it further into her, her walls expanded and she thought he would split her in half. Each inch filled her completely. She came when he was only half way in.

It started with a tremor in her stomach, then spread to her pussy; she shouted as it filled with his cock. Each vibration of her orgasm impaled her further on his pole. With his incredibly strong arms, he lifted her up, then slammed her down to meet his own thrust. He rode her through the orgasm and into another. Her screams of pleasure blended together as he fucked her whole body.

Her vision dimmed and she lost count of the number of times she came. Suddenly, his pace quickened and he plunged himself deep into her. His cock quivered and he exploded into her, filling her whole with his cum.

*

It wasn't cold, not even a little bit. That was the first thing Monique noticed as she stirred to life;

the second, was that she *felt. How many mornings have I spent not feeling anything, not wanting to feel anything?* The loss of her baby, and the events that followed, still existed, they just weren't the all-consuming pain that had smothered her for the last seven years.

Carver rested silently next to her. His muscled chest rose gently up and down. She couldn't help but admire the lines of his nose, his jaw, the way his muscles shifted as he moved. *I can't believe I did that.* Her stomach fluttered at the memory of the night before. *God, I told him everything, and I feel so much better now.* It couldn't be just talking about it. This wasn't the first time she spoke of it. Before she left for the mountains, she saw a psychiatrist and he hadn't been useful at all. But five minutes with

Carver, and a night of passion, and her heart felt light in a way that it hadn't in years.

Kirk whined at her. The little pup trotted onto the sleeping bag and curled up in her bosom. *Something about this wolf, and he is a wolf...* her mind flashed back to Carver saying he wasn't like other men. Well, that was certainly true. The pup snuggled with her before falling to sleep.

"Are you okay?" Carver's voice startled her and she jumped. Kirk didn't seem fazed and continued to sleep.

"What did you do to me?" She looked deep into his brown eyes. A wave of contentment washed over her whole being. The pain in her heart felt like a bad memory. A shadow of the pain it once was.

"I'm sorry Monique, it's part of our gifts, we ease the emotions of others, usually to a place where they're favorable to us. In your case your heart was locked with pain, once I unlocked it, well..." He blushed, she couldn't help but find it adorable.

"What are you?"

He took a deep breath. "You would call me a werewolf, but it's a woefully inaccurate term. I'm a shape shifter, a spirit of the wolf and man together. A guardian of the mountains and of mankind."

What he was saying rang utterly ridiculous in her ears—and she believed every word. "How is this possible, how did you fix this?" She clasped his hand in hers and pulled it to her heart.

"I feel your pain, Monique, as I feel my own. Kirk lost his mother, and he was drawn to you. Your loss called to him, as it called to me. I can feel your emotions almost as I feel my own." He leaned in and gently kissed her lips.

"Kirk is a special pup, he has my gifts, and his mother's, and for that, others want to control him." Absently, she stroked the pup's furry head. Whatever he did, she felt amazing, more alive than she felt in years.

"Thank you," she murmured as she returned his kiss. They lay there, tongues exploring each other's mouths for a while. When they finally broke, Monique felt supercharged. Her whole body was taut, like she just ran a marathon and could run two more.

"Wow," she whispered.

"I've been alive a long time, Monique, and you are a very special woman. I see why he chose you."

She shook her head. "Chose me?"

"You didn't find him by accident, he found you."

Monique wasn't sure what he meant, and her stomach grumbled, interrupting her thoughts.

An hour later, and a good meal of freeze-dried fruit, Monique suited up to go back outside. The storm abated in the night and it was as calm as it was going to be. She zipped up her coat, made sure her pack sat securely on her shoulders, and waved that she was ready.

"We just need to get around the mountain to the other side of Stanton, we have an emergency tunnel for our den. If we get there, we will be safe."

"These other wolves, the ones hunting you and Kirk, won't they just follow us in?"

Carver shook his head, a small smile on his lips. "They have weapons that are formidable, but there aren't enough of them. We would rip them apart in those tunnels."

Before Carver went outside, she watched as he lifted his pant leg. Attached to his leg was some kind of dart she didn't recognize. Fresh blood ran down his leg as he wobbled it.

"I can take this out soon, I think. Once the poison reservoir is empty, I can shift."

"Well, let's go."

The mountain weather during the day was almost the opposite of the night before. Clear skies brought the warm sun to the snow pack. The fresh powder reflected it up, making everything look bright, and very, very white. Monique slid her goggles down over her eyes, then drew her bow. It was a pain to carry while she hiked, but she felt it was worth it if they ran into trouble. She could reliably hit a target one hundred meters away. More if it stood still.

She let Carver lead as they trudged down the mountain. There were no trails to make it easy. The whole journey would be on open fields or dense evergreens. It was slow going for the first few hours, but as they descended further, the mountain levelled somewhat. As the sun rose, the day grew warmer, and she unzipped her coat. Next to her, Kirk whined. She lifted him up and put him in her coat. That seemed to make the little pup happy.

At mid-day, they stopped for a meal. Carver didn't eat. Kirk was more than happy enough to chomp on her jerky. She just fed him the last of her packet when his little ears perked up. Her own hearing seemed overly sensitive this morning. She heard it too, the crunch of a foot on snow.

CHAPTER FIVE

Monique lifted her bow, drew an arrow, and nocked it in one smooth motion. The wolf charged out of the bushes and landed on Carver's back. She let the arrow fly, her hand grabbing the next one before the first one impacted. The arrow caught the black wolf just below the ribs. Carver swung it off his shoulders sending it flying into a tree.

She fired her second arrow—miss. The third was on the string when the wolf charged her. She stepped back as it came at her and let the arrow fly. The flat head was meant for hunting, it was the only thing she used the bow for. The arrows caught the wolf in the roof of his mouth and sunk deep into his brain. He fell in a lump to slide to a stop.

"You okay?" she asked Carver.

"Am I okay? Monique that was amazing. How?"

She hadn't stopped to think, just acted. How had she done that? When she hunted there was no need for such speed, only accuracy. She fired three arrows in three seconds with amazing accuracy.

"I'm not sure, I just did." Monique glanced down to Kirk who whined and wagged his tail.

They quickly covered the wolf with snow; it wouldn't stop his friends from finding him, but it might delay things. Monique moved on autopilot as they resumed their march down the mountain. Something was changing in her and she couldn't put her finger on it. The world seemed brighter, more alive, she could see, smell, hear things that seemed impossible to hear. Though the temperature was still well below freezing, Monique grew increasingly hot as the day went on.

"We need to stop soon. Once the sun goes down, it's going to get very cold," she said. Carver nodded from ahead. She could also see that his leg bled again, which wasn't good. They were being hunted and he left a trail for them to follow.

"Carver, we need to do something about your leg..."

He staggered against a tree. She ran next to him and put her hand on his shoulder. "What's wrong?"

His face dripped with sweat. "The poison... It's run its course, I can shift now. Take Kirk and back away," he grunted. She didn't hesitate. She scooped up the pup and moved behind a tree twenty feet away.

Carver convulsed, he shed his clothes until he stood naked in the snow. He fell to all fours, threw his head back in a scream. Monique watched in awe as his body melted and flowed. Skin and muscles reshaped themselves in a liquid dance that dissolved the man and left the wolf.

"Wow," she said aloud. His head snapped around and yellow eyes narrowed at her. Carver padded over to her and nuzzled her hand for a minute before trotting off in the direction they were headed. Still holding Kirk, she jogged after him.

Landscape moved by at a dizzying pace. Monique heaved huge lungfuls of air as she tried to keep up with Carver. The wolf cut through the forest with a speed no human could match. With sun closing in on the horizon, she finally had to stop. Leaning against a tree to rest, she put Kirk on the ground and then slid down the tree to sit.

Kirk whined at her and pawed her arm. She pulled out the jerky she kept in her sleeve pocket and shared it with him.

Carver came back around a few minutes later, somehow having managed to kill a rabbit in the short time she lost sight of him. He shredded the skin with his teeth and ate.

Monique looked around while they ate. The trees were thinning and if she was right, they would be near the ranger's cabin. They kept it well stocked and accessible. The question she asked herself was, could their pursuers be waiting for them there?

They needed shelter. The storm clouds were back on the horizon. Heavy dark clouds that gathered and pushed toward them. While they sat there, the wind picked up, then snow began to fall.

"I don't know if you can understand me like this, but we need to head to the ranger's cabin. Follow me." She grunted as she stood, her legs were sore, but she could do it. The cabin was maybe a mile away. Kirk trotted behind her, scrambling over one obstacle after another. Carver kept his distance and followed her from behind. She couldn't shake the feeling that he was stalking her. Not that he was, but having a wolf at her back triggered primordial instincts to run.

Monique marvelled at the forest as they moved through it. The sound of birds, too distant to see, echoed in her ears. The slightest movement of a leaf drew her attention. She put Kirk down for a moment to kneel beside him.

"What's happening to me, pup?" She said as she absently scratched his neck. Since she woke up, the world seemed... different. A snap of a twig brought her head around. The world faded, the edges blurred, and her vision shot through the forest. A large man with a scarred face stepped through the woods. Cradled in his arm was a hunting rifle.

He's following us.

"Carver, move!" she yelled. The wolf shot off like a bullet. Monique scooped up Kirk with one arm and tucked him in her jacket as she ran.

"We need to get to the ranger station, we can call for help from there," she said as she darted in between trees and over fallen logs. Her feet crunched in the ankle-deep snow. Off to her right, in the direction of their destination, she heard the howl of wolves. She skidded to a stop, lungs gasping for air.

"They're trying to cut us off," she told Kirk. Ahead she could see Carver's sleek form rounding back toward her. On her knees, she pulled out the map. Normally she stuck to the high altitudes, and only came down to go to town. Unfolded, the map took up a square foot, and showed the topography of everything within ten square miles of the cabin. She quickly estimated where they were, and where the ranger's cabin was. The wolves to the south were coming directly up the trail that led to safety. To their north, a sheer cliff blocked them in, and to the east, the direction they needed to go, a ravine blocked the way.

But... the ravine isn't impassable. She recalled seeing it once. When she first moved here, there were stone fingers that criss-crossed it here and there. Of course, it was hundreds of feet down to the bottom.

Better than being eaten alive by wolves or shot by scarface.

"Carver, here boy," she whistled. The wolf trotted over to her. She pointed on the map where they needed to go. He looked to her, she couldn't tell what he was thinking behind those yellow eyes.

She pointed again. He took off in the right direction. The map folded up easy enough, and slid back inside her jacket along with Kirk. Before she left, she took a pull of her water, ate a bite of jerky, and made sure her boots were tied. Falling off a cliff because she was hungry or her boots weren't tied seemed a ridiculous way to go. The howl of the wolves, much closer this time, inspired her to run on.

The snow gradually disappeared as they descended at a rapid pace. Rocky crags and outcroppings replaced the woods. Her ears were filled with the sound of rushing water beating against rocks. The waterfall that came off the cliff took her breath away. Five hundred feet up, it rained down snow melt into the ravine. The ravine itself lay a hundred feet across, and at least two hundred feet down. She surveyed it from the edge, taking a moment to catch her breath before finding a way across.

Carver sat on his haunches beside her, his tongue hanging out as he panted. Even now, being chased by people and wolves, she couldn't help but think of the previous night, and how it made her insides melt just imagining him inside her again.

A shadow passed over them dropping the temperature by ten degrees. It was a stark reminder of what would happen if they didn't get to that cabin when the sun dropped behind the mountain. She held her hand up, horizontally, fingers together, with her pointer just below the sun. *Thirty minutes, tops. Then it drops to below zero.*

Almost on cue, the wind picked up and blew a stiff, cold breeze across her face. The sweat on her forehead froze immediately. It was time to go. A few hundred feet down river, a geological formation crossed the chasm. The base of it lay twenty feet from the top, and it stretched almost entirely across the river. The other side of the chasm rested thirty feet down from the upward side. If she could get to the stone bridge, she could maybe make the jump to the other side.

That's a big maybe. With no other options, she patted Carver on the head, and pointed where she wanted to go. He galloped down there instantly. A bullet skipped off the ground where he sat a split second before.

Monique whipped around to face the west, with the sun in her eyes though, she couldn't see anything. Wherever he was, it was past his range to hit a moving target. She ran southward along the ridge. Another bullet hit the stone behind her.

"Carver, move!" she screamed as yet another bullet hit the ground. The finger of stone that crossed the chasm was below her now. She hit the quick release on her pack and tossed it down to the stone. It caught on a crop of stone that blended into the rock and went spinning off into the river below.

"Shit!"

That was all her gear, gun, sleeping bag, extra food. *I'm dead if we don't get there.* Carver leaped past her onto the rocks, his paws scraping for traction as he hit. He made it, though. The wolf took a tentative step and then headed for the other side. One thing she was certain of, she couldn't stay here. Any second a bullet would hit her in the back. Not wanting to risk her bow she pulled it over her head. Turning around to go feet first she knelt down and dropped her legs over the side.

A cloud passed in front of the sun and she could make out Scarface. He was close, only seven hundred feet away now, he raised his rifle. She dropped. The bullet sparked off the stone where her head had been a moment before.

She hit the ground hard. Her arms pinwheeled as she fell backwards scrambling for traction. She couldn't find purchase as she felt herself sliding over the edge. Kirk jumped out of her jacket as she went over. At the last second her fingers found a ledge and she grabbed it. Everything stopped. She hung off the stone bridge by one arm. Kirk's little fur-covered face above her, and a nearly two hundred foot drop to the icy water, below her.

"Okay, you can do this," she grunted as she swung her hand over to find a hold. Something jutted out she couldn't see, but she felt it. Her fingers wrapped around it and she didn't let go. Sweat beaded in her hair and temples. Her arms ached from the strain of holding her up. With nothing to push off of with her feet, she had to rely entirely on upper body strength to get to the top. Inch by gruelling inch, she pulled herself up. Each second that passed she knew brought death that much closer.

Finally, she was up high enough to put her whole arm over the top, and one foot grabbed hold of the bridge itself. With one last heave she rolled on to the flat surface, her bow digging painfully in her back. Heaving, but unable to rest, she dragged herself up. The narrow rocky bridge wasn't meant to be walked on. Only inches wide in the middle, it stretched across the ravine like a horizontal stalagmite.

Kirk trotted away, deftly walking on the ridge seemingly unaware that he could fall. Monique followed after him. Her boots fought for traction with each step. The closer to the middle she got, the less surface area she had to walk on. Carver was already on the far bank, waiting for them. She dare not take her eyes off the stone lest she fall, and she didn't think her arms had it in them to pull her up again.

She tried to stifle the terror she felt, to push past the thought of the cold death that waited for her below. She wanted to scream, to cry, to curl up in a little ball and forget this was happening. But she couldn't. Years of living just to survive ingrained in her a desperate need to soldier on. And even though she felt she could have more to live for now, that urgent need to survive wouldn't simply go away.

The center of the bridge loomed. She knelt down to cross it on all fours. Sliding her weight along without breaking contact with the ground let her cross without falling. Behind her, she heard the sound of a bolt being cycled. Brass clinked off the stone.

"That's far enough lady."

Without moving her body, she turned her head. Fifty feet behind her, and on the ridge, stood Scarface, his rifle pointed right at her.

*

"Bring me the pup and I'll let you live," the Scarface man behind her growled. Kirk hid, just inches from her. Carver couldn't reach them without being shot. It was all on Monique. If she relaxed her legs, even a bit, she would slip and fall. All that held her to the thin piece of stone was her thigh muscles. She looked down again. The river wound down the ravine below them. It wasn't deep though, if she fell from this height she would hit the bottom with enough force to kill her.

"I've no problem shooting a woman. You'd be the second this week." He laughed.

Her eyes shot up to Carver. Even at this distance, she could see the sorrow fill his yellow eyes. *Why didn't he say anything?* A wave of guilt swept through her. After all, she practically seduced him. And he was still mourning his wife.

No, she said to herself. There was only one thing to do.

"Kirk, come here boy," she made little kissing noises with her lips. Carver jumped up, but Scarface shot off a round at him, forcing him back into cover. Kirk trotted to her, his little face trusting of her.

She pushed back the guilt she felt for what she was about to do. The hunter left her no choice though.

"You want him..." she held him up above her head before stuffing him inside her jacket. "Come get him," she looked to Carver, smiled, and let herself fall off the bridge.

"No!" Scarface screamed as she fell.

The wind rushed past her face. She curled up into a ball, hoping that when she hit, her body would at least protect Kirk and let him live. Accepting her fate she closed her eyes. Air flowed around her, she felt at peace, and strangely light as she rushed through the air.

A long moment passed and nothing happened. She didn't impact with the ground, there was no sharp, watery death. Afraid to open her eyes lest she do it a mere second before she hit the ground, she squeezed them even tighter. She could still feel Kirk in her arms, the wind rushing by her. The sound of the river faded below her. She opened her eyes.

The water rushed by underneath her. But not *toward* her.

"What," she said, startled. Words didn't reach her ears. The sharp cry of a hawk drowned her out. Air rushed around her. She looked left and right. Her body was gone, white feathery wings with brown tops were to her sides. Where she had feet, she now had talons, which held Kirk tightly by the scruff. She screamed.

The hawks piercing cry filled the canyon. *I'm a hawk... this is a delusion, the kind you get before you die.* Instinctively, she beat her wings. An updraft caught her and she rode it above the canyon. Leaning to the left, she banked to the east and felt her body respond. A sharp crack echoed up. She looked down at the source. She could see Scarface in brilliant detail. Even though he was hundreds of feet away. Another crack. *He's shooting at me!*

She tucked her wings in and dove for the ground. Carver ran below her, almost in slow motion compared to her. She passed above him, her wings folded and her beak pointed at the tree line to the south. Without thinking she spread her wings wide. The air caught her feathers. The wind break brought her to a stop and she dropped to the ground. No longer a hawk, but a woman. She cradled Kirk in her arms. The cold wind sliced through her naked body.

Everything felt different. The wind felt like home to her, it pulled at her to go up. To soar among the clouds. Kirk yipped as Carver came to a halt. He licked his son before turning his yellow eyes on Monique.

"What happened?" she said, still breathing heavy from her flight.

The wolf didn't answer.

The sun sank below the mountain to the west, and they were out of time. With no other options she headed for the cabin. Naked and freezing, she made her way across the rocky ground, step by step.

Crossing the ravine shaved hours off their trip. Despite the dropping temperature, Monique managed to keep walking. She knew the cabin couldn't be far. Her hands shook with each step. The numbing cold spread in from her extremities. Her teeth clattered and she couldn't make them stop. *I'm going to die out here.* Carver growled ahead of her. She couldn't focus on him, everything seemed hazy and indistinct. Warm fur pressed against her legs, she hadn't realized she'd stopped moving. He pushed until she put one foot in front of the other.

The darkness enveloped her. Without a moon, the night seemed black and forbearing. Every few seconds Carver would stop and push her, she couldn't feel her feet. She stumbled, and tried to reach out to right herself. Her face slammed into wood with a jolt.

The cabin. Get in.

The ranger's cabin opened before her. She knew she needed to get warm, but she couldn't make her body respond. A blanket-less bed stood empty in the corner. The fire was unlit. She managed to stumble to the bed before she collapsed. Carver hopped up with her, carrying Kirk by the scruff of the neck. His body generated a tremendous amount of heat. The wolf draped his body on hers, resting his head on her neck. Weakly, she reached out to him to hold his fur in her hands.

"Good boy," she murmured before darkness claimed her.

CHAPTER SIX

The sky flew by above her. Clouds so close she could reach out and touch them. She looked down to the ground, it moved in a blur beneath. Other birds chased her, but none could catch her. She was pure speed. Her piercing cry filled the sky. Up in the heavens, Monique felt invincible. She closed her eyes and let the wind ruffle her feathers. When she opened them the sky was gone, and she smelled bacon.

"You're awake! I was starting to worry," Carver said from behind her.

Monique pulled the warm blanket up to her chin. Did she have to move?

"I've got breakfast here for you if you're hungry." Okay, she did have to move. Her stomach threatened open revolt if she didn't. Wrapped in the blanket, she was still naked underneath, she moved to the small card table that served as the cabin's dining table. Carver laid out a plate with eggs, bacon, bread, and cheese, along with orange juice.

"Where did you find all this?" She asked as she took a bite of the bacon. Her mouth watered from the taste.

"They have a freezer out back that runs off solar power; everything we need was in it." He smiled as she ate. She couldn't help but notice something in his eyes. Suddenly, she felt very under-dressed as he gazed at her. The memory of their passion sent little shock waves on her skin, and made her moist in all the right places. But there was something else in his gaze, something reverent.

"What?" she said finally after a long drink of juice.

"Do you remember?"

Of course she remembered. She could hardly forget falling to her death only to be saved by shifting into a hawk.

"Yes, but I'm not sure what happened. It's like a dream, or a memory of a dream. Did I really turn into…?"

"A hawk?" he finished for her.

Kirk licked her ankles. She reached down to pick him up, feeding him bits of bacon off her plate as she worked on the eggs.

"Yeah, I did, didn't I? Did you do that to me when we..."

"No. Even if I wanted to I couldn't make you a wolf, let alone a hawk. Up until yesterday I thought us wolves were it. We..." he paused. She could tell he wanted to say something more, but he was holding back. She finished her breakfast in silence. Interrupted only by Kirk whining for food. She gladly shared her bacon with the little pup. She needed Carver to trust her, to believe in her. Also, she admitted, she needed to know what he knew. Was it permanent? Could she do it again?

A sigh escaped her lips as she glanced over at him. He'd found a pair of sweat pants somewhere in the cabin. She admired the way his muscles rippled together as he walked, stood, talked. Everything. He took her plate to the sink. There were dishes from before they came. She watched while he worked. The rough fabric of the blanket rubbed painfully against her swollen nipples. Her flesh tingled with desire as she daydreamed about their night together.

Kirk leaped off the table to hide under the bed. *What's wrong with me?* She didn't know. Her stomach ached from desire, her thighs wet from her need. She cast the blanket aside. He froze when she ran her hands over his shoulders and down his sides, around his waist. As her hands moved down under the pants she pressed her tits into his back, while her hands found his cock. She purred as it stirred to life beneath her touch. Gently, she pulled on it, coaxing it to full size. He moaned under her touch.

"Monique..." He tried to speak, but she ran her fingers down the length to the crown before twisting them to the side. His hands gripped the counters. He was a big man, and she easily slipped around under his arms to face him. Her lips brushed against his, she opened her mouth letting her tongue out to trace the corners of his lips. She slipped her hands down to rub his erection through the thin sweat pants. His hips moved ever so slightly. She couldn't help but smile.

Her tongue slipped into his mouth and he moaned into hers as she worked his cock. He trembled under her. She broke their kiss and moved her lips down his neck. His hands still held a death grip on the counter, even as she sunk down to suck one nipple in her mouth. He hissed. Lower still she went and as she descended she pushed his sweat pants down around his penis.

On her knees, and face to face with it, Monique gasped. She hadn't dreamed such a thing existed. Not only was it massive... *it's beautiful.* She lifted it to lick the underside, sending Carver into a fit of grunts. She ran her tongue down to his two large balls. Gently, she sucked one into her mouth. His hair was fine and sparse like a Native American's. His red tinged skin and high cheekbones suddenly made sense to her.

Her hand moved up and down his shaft, twisting at the head to stimulate it. She opened her mouth to suck the side of his cock and ran her tongue all the way to the tip. She let out a breath, it was a moment of panic for her. This was new territory and she didn't want to disappoint him. Forming an "o" with her mouth, she gently slid the tip of his cock between her lips. He groaned so loud she worried he was hurt, until his hand grasped the back of her head and pushed her down. The head of his cock slid between her lips. She swirled her tongue around it before sucking on it to pull it in further.

Her body responded to him. His other hand roamed down to her hard nipples, twisting and pulling on them, sending little bolts of pleasure to her brain. Her pussy dripped with need. Deciding to go for it, she pulled him into her mouth as far as she could. His cock pushed against her throat. She pulled out to the very end then slid it back again. Each movement followed by one hand, while with the other she squeezed and tugged on his balls.

His grip on her head tightened, the cock in her mouth swelled and he pushed her down hard. The tip hit the back of her throat and wedged itself in. He pushed her up against the counter and groaned as his body tensed. Monique let out a soft moan as his cock exploded. Hot semen gushed forth. She gulped down the first wave of the salty fluid, and the second, her cheeks billowed on the third, by the fourth it leaked out between her lips but she worked hard to swallow it all.

She felt the last bit flow down her throat. He slowly slid his cock out of her mouth, she kept her lips pressed tightly around it to drink up all of his cum. It popped out of her mouth, a line of his semen stretched from her lips to his dick. She looked up to him and smiled, his eyes beamed back love.

Suddenly, he lifted her up. A squeak escaped her lips as he pulled her into a kiss. She wrapped her legs around his waist. His hands explored her back as their tongues fought in a mock battle that both were willing to lose. She moaned into his mouth as his cock rubbed against her wetness. They couldn't contain their lust as he pushed her up against the wall. He found her pussy and groaned with pleasure as he forced the head past her lips.

"Oh fuck," she moaned. His cock filled her, more than that, it *fulfilled* her. He expanded her insides and touched every inch of her. Tears of joy rolled down her cheeks as he pulled out, then pushed in. His rhythm ignited her desire as it forced her nipples to rub against him. She moaned and thrashed as he fucked her against the wall. Their wails of passion filled the air when she finally came in a thunderous scream of ecstasy.

As she shuddered and came down off her orgasm, Carver continued to pump away inside of her. His breathing picked up with his speed. She whimpered from the pleasure with each thrust. She felt his cock expand inside her. He grunted and thrust one last time with all his strength. Semen burst forth to fill her warm pussy with its hot juice. Carver continued to thrust with a primal need to sink his cock as far in her as possible. And to pump as much of his cum into her.

They moaned together as they slid down the wall to sit on the floor. She rested her head on his shoulders as she recovered her breath.

"Oh wow, can we do that again?" she whispered sleepily.

"As many times as you like. Forever and ever," he murmured.

*

Carefully, as not to wake him, Monique disentangled herself from Carver's limbs. Her own legs were unsteady as she tried to stand. *What is wrong with me?* Seven years she lived on that mountain, not even so much as thinking of men. Now, she slept with a stranger twice in two days. And not just sex, her whole body ached from the fucking he gave her. Saliva filled her mouth at the thought of the orgasms that dotted her memory. Never in her whole life had she imagined sex could be that good.

She downed a glass of water. Followed by another. Outside, the weather beat against the cabin in a relentless gale. The people who were after him certainly couldn't move in this weather. The snow swirled from the wind, she couldn't even see ten feet out the window. Still, something tingled between her shoulders, something not right.

Kirk's whining snapped her head around. The little pup crawled out from beneath the bed toward her. The lights in the cabin flickered. *No, not the lights, my vision.* Kirk was closer now, sitting on his haunches looking at her. Pain sprang from her gut so fast it dropped her to one knee.

"What..." she panted. Carver stirred from the bed. Sweat dripped down her face to pool on the floor. The pain in her stomach spread to her limbs. She gagged as bile built up in her throat.

"Let it happen Monique, trying to fight it will only make it worse," came his soothing voice.

Fight it? Fight what?

"It... HURTS," she screamed. Her hands slipped and she collapsed on the floor. Convulsions racked her body; she couldn't see, couldn't breathe.

"I'm sorry, Kirk needs a protector, and he chose you. I should have warned you this would happen. But... I thought you might run," he whispered to her.

The world fell into blurry, pain-filled sections. Spasms sent her tumbling on the floor. Her skin burned and felt tight. She screamed again as her back convulsed. The terrible sound of skin ripping reached her ears, and she realized it was her skin.

"I'm sorry, Monique, this was the only way."

She screamed again, but her howl came out as a growl. She stumbled to the door and collapsed against it. Her hands wouldn't turn the knob, she had to get out though, get away from him, from the pain. She tried again, the door budged, the wind caught it and slammed it against the outside wall. Unable to stand she tumbled through it, out into the snow.

Twenty feet from the door she couldn't see, the pain rippled through her. She dropped again, heaving up her food. The pain was so intense, only a dull ring filled her ears, she couldn't hear the storm, or see the snow, or feel the cold. *He did this to me, made me one of him. Has he be lying to me since the beginning? Oh god the things I let him do to me.* Sorrow from the betrayal welled up in her, but was quickly pushed aside from the agony her body went through. Unable to take it any longer, she collapsed into the snow, curled around herself to hug away the pain.

The sun woke her, not the cold. She yawned, a long, lanky yawn that cleared the fog away from her mind. *I should be dead.* She wasn't, though, and the cold didn't seem to bother her. Her limbs felt awkward as she tried to stand. Her whole body shook from the exertion. She wobbled up to stand on four limbs. Looking down, she saw paws with white fur, but not the paws of a wolf. Sharp, curved claws came out of these. The white fur only interrupted by dark spots. Tentatively she took a step, then another. Her back and ass felt weighed down. She tried to turn her head to see it, but her body responded by turning. Several seconds of chasing her tail and she stopped. She wasn't a wolf, nor a hawk. *I'm a leopard. A snow leopard. But... I was a hawk, and now this... am I dreaming?* Briefly she wondered if she were dead in the snow, and this was somehow a dream before dying. The sharp crack of a rifle shattered that illusion.

Snow beside her exploded with the impact. She jumped sideways, clearing ten feet of ground. She couldn't tell where the bullet came from, but she didn't need to, she just ran. Her paws glided across the fresh snow, she felt her tail swivel to offset her weight as she turned to dive behind a tree. Another crack. The bark disintegrated in a shower of splinters.

He's out there, somewhere to the north.

She pivoted again, running as fast as her legs would take her. The ground passed by in a blur. Rocks swept up and passed her, another crack. Sparks exploded from the rock. Each shot gave her more information on where he was. Her large paws allowed her to cut corners in the snow and on the rocks. Another shot. *Got you.*

One last correction and she charged with everything she had. She felt stronger than she ever had. The distance narrowed with each stride. A huge rock ahead offered the perfect vantage point. Lungs barely bothered from the exertion, she slowed down to creep up to the outcropping. His smell wafted over on the breeze. She could hear his breathing. At the top of the rock, she knelt down to shimmy along the last little bit. Head resting on her paws she looked down. Behind a tree, not twenty feet away, a man knelt with a rifle. It wasn't Scarface, she didn't know who he was. But he smelled like trouble.

She leaped. He turned as she flew, but it wasn't fast enough. She hit him claws out, and her fangs tore a huge chunk out of one arm. He screamed and thrashed, sending her flying. She flipped in the air, landed on her feet, and roared.

The man ripped his coat off and roared back. In an instant, his countenance shifted and he howled at her from the form of a wolf, not a man. He was bigger than her. Two hundred pounds at least. He shifted to his side, trying to get her to turn around, but she was having none of it. With a growl, she bared her fangs, ears lying flat against her head, tail straight up. He darted forward to nip at her, claws flashed and she batted his head aside. Not wanting to waste the opportunity, she pounced. Her fangs found his throat and latched on. The wolf spasmed and he flew off the ground trying to buck her off or flip her over. She felt his skin tear under her as he shifted his weight so that he was on top of her. Fangs snapped inches from her. On her back now, she brought her rear claws up and shredded his belly. Now he wasn't trying to get the upper hand so much as get away. Warm blood splashed across her coat as she tore into him. He jerked against her hard, she flew away smashing into a tree. Monique was back on her feet in an instant, tail straight back to give her the most weight. The wolf took one step toward her, then collapsed on the ground. Its pitiful whine pulled at her heart as he died.

Monique spat out the chunk of flesh that she tore from his throat. She wasn't sure he was dead, and didn't want to make the mistake thinking he was. Her paw batted his head aside a few times but he didn't move. Satisfied, she turned to leave.

If he knew where I was... then they know where Carver is!

CHAPTER SEVEN

The flames reached the sky above. The intense heat melted the snow for twenty feet around the cabin. Monique looked on from the tree line, not wanting to give herself away. Three men, all dressed in hunting gear with rifles and packs watched the cabin burn. She couldn't smell anything other than the burning wood, plastic, and synthetics that the blaze consumed. Her nose twitched, looking for any sign of Carver and Kirk. What she didn't smell was burning meat. Whatever happened, they weren't in that cabin.

One of them turned to the tree line. He looked up and down before walking toward her. She sunk back into the shadows. *Did he see me?* A few steps into the woods he stopped, looked left and right, then unzipped his pants.

He wore a large knife around his belt, and set his rifle down a few feet away. Monique circled around behind him, her cat's stealth unsurpassed in her element. What she needed, though, was to talk to him. She padded directly behind him, the stream of his piss hid her approach. With her eyes on his back she willed herself to change. Hoping it wasn't the painful ordeal of before. Her vision shifted as she went from cat's eyes to human's, her head raised, and her limbs filled out. In seconds she knelt behind him, naked, cold, but very much human.

As fast as she could, she leaped at him. Her left arm went around his throat while her right hand snapped up the knife. He froze as the cold blade slipped under his dick, sharp side up. He hissed. But he didn't move.

"Where's Carver?"

The wolf, she could smell it on him now that she was close to him, didn't respond.

"You have a bitch at home, you want pups? Talk or I cut it off, and somehow I don't think it will grow back."

The man swallowed hard. "They took him and the pup to town."

"Why?"

When he didn't answer, she lifted the blade up. He raised on his toes, but said nothing.

"Fine." She slowly stuck out her tongue and ran it up his neck to his ear. His cock jerked in response.

"Jesus fucking Christ, we needed Carver to control the pup, fuck, stop!" He screamed. *Carver said Kirk was special, but how special? Was he telling the truth when he said he hadn't done this to her? He certainly seemed like he knew what was going on.*

"Jake, you okay back there?" A voice came from the clearing.

"Tell 'em you tripped or I give you the blow job of your life," she whispered menacingly. His cock stirred on the knife and he whimpered.

"I'm fine, just startled by something."

She pulled the blade off of him. He let out a breath and she struck his head with the pommel. He sank to his knees. She hit him again and he was out. It wouldn't take long for the other hunters to find him. Seconds ticked by while she evaluated her options. Town stood eleven miles away at the bottom of the mountain. In the past when she went there, she rode her four wheeler. That was back at her cabin, and these men weren't likely to let her ride out of here. If they took Carver and Kirk there, that meant they had a vehicle of some kind not far away.

The hunter was a big man, big enough she couldn't easily roll him over. She grabbed his rifle, the ammo pouch on his belt, and the knife before running back into the woods. Screaming followed her not thirty seconds later. *How do I get to the town like this?*

Monique ran until she couldn't hear them any more. Her lungs burned from the exertion. The mid-morning sun warmed her skin, but it was still cold on the mountain. And she had no clothes.

She stopped to sit on a log for a minute and think. Since Carver came into her life, she'd been reacting. *If you're honest with yourself, you've been reacting for seven years now.* It was time to stop reacting, and start acting. How was the question. Her new found nature was a mystery to her. Did Carver do it to her? It sure seemed like he knew something the night before. Or had he simply sensed it about her? In just a few days, the world had flipped on its side and everything was different.

The sharp cry of a hawk brought her attention upward. He circled above, head darting back and forth as he searched for prey. She'd done that.

Without thinking, without hesitating, thrown herself off that log—knowing she would die—and then... she was a hawk.

It's Kirk, Carver said he was special. From the moment you found him things have been stirring in you. The feelings she buried for so long had welled up in her the moment she rescued the little pup. The moment she *decided* to rescue him and not turn her back on him.

She looked up into the sky, closed her eyes, took a deep breath, and leaped. The wind rushed under her wings as she beat them hard against the air. Her eyes popped open and she could see for miles. A glance told her she had the wings and talons of a hawk. Her snowy white feathers caught the heat as it reflected off the ground, and with no effort she raised into the sky with it. Five hundred feet flew by, then a thousand. The world looked small and pristine from up here.

It would be easy to get lost in it. To let the glory of flight, the feeling of the wind over her feathers, consume her. All too easy. She rejoiced in it for a moment. Then let her mind focus back on the task at hand. There was only one trail down that was big enough for vehicles. Even if they weren't on it, she knew where the road was. With a mere flick of her feathers she banked hard right, tucked her wings in, and zoomed off in the direction of town.

When she was a little girl she read that hawks could reach two hundred miles an hour in a dive. She decided to see if it was true.

*

Carver growled at Brennan from across the bed of the truck.

"Oh stop your complaining, he's alive—for now." Brennan motioned to Kirk, in a small dog traveller made for road trips. "If you're smart, you will not misbehave, I don't want him hurt, but I only need him alive, not in one piece."

Carver could barely contain himself. His growl resonated on a subsonic level sending the two men on either side of him into fits of concern. They glanced at Brennan, then back to Carver. There was power in an Alpha, not just as a leader, and they felt it on him.

"Calm down, he won't do anything to risk his precious pup." Brennan waved around the dead man switch he held in his hand. It was tied to a small battery pack that would release fifty thousand volts on the pup, and likely stop his heart.

"See, he calms."

"This won't work Brennan, he's already chosen, and it wasn't me," Carver said smugly.

"The bitch?" Brennan smiled. "She's a fine piece of ass, but I'm afraid she's dead by now. No, it will be me Carver, or I will kill you so slowly, it will take weeks for you to die."

*

The sky rushed by. Monique lifted her wings and the world came to a crashing halt. Her two hundred a mile an hour dive took her down the mountain and over the town in less than a minute. Now, she circled lazily above the town, her sharp hawk's eyes seeing everything. Rocky terrain gave way to sloping hills and flat, grass-filled fields. At first there were only a few houses, but as she flew closer to the town proper, a small city sprung up in the foot hills.

Compared to New Orleans, it was a hamlet. Only a half dozen major buildings, and twice as many minor ones. Most of the people who lived in town existed off the income of the mountains. Tourists, government employees, hikers, environmentalists, all of them needed access, and when they got here, they needed supplies. The largest building stood flat against a small hill—the courthouse.

Monique circled the town once; very little, if anything moved. The roof of the courthouse came into view as she glided closer to the town. A man, rugged, with an orange hunters vest knelt behind the statue of justice. She focused her vision on him. He carried a rifle just like the rest of the hunters. With a flap of her wings, she gained a few hundred feet. Twisting her body she angled up and behind the building. The updraft carried her without her having to move. Once she was past the town she turned back to the roof. It was easily a half mile away. She folded in her wings and traded altitude for speed.

At the last moment, she triggered her change. Monique's heel slammed into his lower back with tremendous force. She felt the bones break in his spine. He collapsed, gasping for a breath that wouldn't come. She knelt on his neck until he stopped moving.

The rumble of a diesel truck interrupted her kill. At the end of town, an open bed truck turned the last corner. Her vision swam as the town rushed by and she could see Carver in the bed of the truck. It came to a clunking halt outside the sheriff's office.

Figures. The whole damn town seems to be in on it.

That left her in a bind. How many people were against them, and why? Why was Kirk important enough to kill for? She quickly searched the man she killed. His clothes were too big for her, and his outfit stunk of death. The rifle would make too much noise if she used it, as would the handgun he carried. No, she was going to have to do this quietly; if there was a fight, they had too many people. She ducked down to the ledge and gave the town one more sweep, she spied what she needed

It took her five minutes to get down from the courthouse by scaling the drain in the back, another ten and she was behind the only store in town. The door that faced the same cliff as the courthouse was locked. A growl escaped her lips. She put her shoulder to it and increased pressure. The metal resisted for a moment, then protested, and finally gave with a wrench. Monique paused for a moment to make sure no one heard. Once she was in, she closed the door and leaned a rack against it to warn her if anyone came in.

You realize you just pushed in a metal fire door. Right? Something deep inside her had changed, there was no doubt. Gone was the girl hiding from her emotions, she was driven by them now. She felt a deep need to protect Kirk, to help Carver, and stop these people from hurting either. She wouldn't call it love, but it was like that. Her heart raced at the passion she shared with him, and she could only imagine what her future would be like, when every night was like that. The twinge of pleasure, followed by the moistening of her nether regions reminded her to focus, now wasn't the time to get lost in lust.

The General Store carried everything she needed, clothes, boots, a jacket, and a big knife. As she was about to leave, she noticed the stack of propane cans in the back. An evil grin spread across her face.

The sheriff's office didn't have the cliff behind it. A large, empty lot separated it from its nearest building. It was ideal for seeing someone coming from any direction. Two men on the roof, one who glanced at the sky every few minutes, reinforced their preparedness. Monique slid around back, opposite the building, behind the little diner. She could peek her eyes out and see across the street. At some point, the truck had been moved, and she could see through the picture window with the gold badge painted on it.

Scarface looked out the window right at her. She froze, terrified he saw her, but knowing sudden movement would draw his attention. When he didn't react, she moved her head as far behind the corner of the building as she could and still see. He looked up and down the street before turning around.

She checked her pilfered watch. *Any second now.*

The fire alarm from the store split the air as it wailed. Oily black smoke began to drift up from the back where the propane tanks were stored. A muffled explosion told her that it reached the rest of the building, and then the blaze started in earnest. After a few moments, one of them checked his radio, then climbed down. The town was suddenly full of people running to see what happened, and if they could help. A population this small didn't have a dedicated fire department, it was something that everyone did.

She waited for her moment then charged across the street. One more person trying to see what happened. The remaining sentry never looked her way as she got to the sheriff's office. She scooted along the edge to the back, the jail cell had an open, barred window. The sound of flesh on flesh echoed through it. Almost afraid to look, she hesitantly cast her eyes over the edge.

Carver sat, zip tied to a chair, as one of Scarface's henchmen hit him in the face repeatedly.

CHAPTER EIGHT

"How do I become the guardian?" Brennan asked again. When Carver didn't answer he nodded to his associate.

Whack.

"What does he use to choose who it shall be?"

Whack.

"How long does the guardian retain their abilities?"

Whack.

"Damn it, Carver, stop being so stubborn and tell me something!"

Whack.

Carver's face felt like one pile of pain. His right eye puffed shut, and his lips were bleeding. The torture hadn't even really begun. All he could do was buy Monique time to get Kirk and get away. It wasn't as if he could answer any of the questions Brennan asked. Carver had assumed that Kirk's mother would be the guardian. When she died, he figured that was it. But now... now he knew it was always meant to be Monique. Despite the pain, he smiled, cracked lips bleeding. She was a magnificent woman, and Kirk couldn't have chosen a better one.

"I would tell you Brennan, but you wouldn't believe me, you think Kirk is something to be controlled, and I'm telling you, his power is not for those who seek it, but those who need it." The man's fist broke his nose this time. Pain blossomed in his forehead and he felt blood flow freely down his chest.

"Idiot, never break their nose unless you're done with 'em, we don't want him dead, go get a rag," Brennan yelled at his partner. The man nodded and went to the bathroom.

"It's hard to find good help. I had to scrounge every lone wolf in North America, but they all want the promise, Carver, the promise that being a wolf can fulfill." He pulled out his knife, a long black blade with a thin edge. "And you're going to help me do that."

"Ha, Brennan, you never understood what pack life was about. You saw it as your personal harem, nothing more than a place for you to fuck."

Brennan's face clouded with anger. "Is that why you kicked me out? You wanted all the women for yourself. Jealous of my prowess? They begged me to fuck them, every one of those bitches, they begged for it."

Carver shook his head. "You're deluded. I didn't kick you out, they all came to me, they told me what you did, and that if you didn't go, they would. You are just a man, Brennan, another wolf among hundreds. You can't have kids, they can. You honestly think your sexual satisfaction even played a factor in the decision? You are nothing. And you proved it with this."

Brennan lost it. His blade came down hard on Carvers leg. He slammed his fist into Carver's face, once, twice, three times, over and over again.

Thank god, if he kills me, he will keep Kirk safe as long as he thinks he can be the guardian.

A tremendous roar shook the building. The wall behind Carver collapsed in a shower of dust and debris. Something massive knocked Carver's chair over, he fell on his shoulder with a grunt.

"What the fuck?!" yelled Brennan.

Carver's vision cleared and he saw what caused it. A polar bear swept past him, one massive paw batting Brennan aside like a rag doll. His man came out from the back room, eyes wide with fright. He pulled his pistol and opened fire. The bear roared in his direction, massive white teeth larger than a forearm. The gun clicked empty and the bear wasn't even hurt. It looked at the man before her massive fangs came down on his shoulder. He screamed as blood spurted from the wound. She shook him back and forth letting him fly into the wall.

"Monique, look out!"

Brennan glanced at him, eyes wide with anger. "She's the guardian? *Her*?! Damn you Carver, damn you to hell." He ripped off his shirt and in the space of a moment shifted to a large wolf with one mauled eye. He growled at the bear, the bear was unimpressed. The two collided in the center of the room. Kirk's cage slammed against the wall and the small gate opened. The little pup skittered through the room to his father.

"Run, boy, run!"

The pup yipped, then set about chewing on the zip ties that bound Carver to the chair. The bear roared with pain as Brennan latched onto her hind legs. The bear's form filled the room. She couldn't maneuver well, or turn fast. Carver watched in awe as she threw herself out of the window. Her massive weight carried Brennan with her. Once on the street, the bear shook him off her leg, sending him sprawling.

People screamed at the sudden appearance of a polar bear. Even shifters feared the mighty hunters from the north. Carver's mind was numb, he didn't know she could do that. His hand sprung free; Kirk set to work on the last one while he tried to free his leg.

*

Monique wasn't sure what happened, but once she saw Carver getting pummelled, she saw red. Now she was on the street, in a wide open space, with the paws of the largest bear she had ever seen. Two wolves joined Scarface, they circled her, looking for a weak spot. Getting out in the open helped her, but it also helped them. She took a step forward, swiping at the closest wolf. He jumped back. They were agile and fast, she was slow and powerful. But there were more of them. Pain lanced through her haunches as a wolf latched on. She turned, and more pain from her left side. She lunged forward, clipping one, sending him sprawling. Something jumped on her back and bit her neck. They were going for the kill. She got her teeth around something and bit down hard. A howl of pain filled the street before sharply ending when she crunched down with her massive jaws. She spat the limp wolf out.

A shot rang out. Pain blossomed in her side. Queasiness filled her stomach and made her vision swim. Her paws wavered and suddenly she was a woman again, naked, and kneeling on the street.

The wolves all growled as one by one they shifted back to human. Four of them now, men all, with large muscular bodies and huge cocks, they surrounded her. Evil grins split their faces. Brennan was the largest of them all.

"She's mine first, then you can take your turns with her, or go all at once, but she pays for what she's done."

His member twitched with excitement. Monique growled with the rage in her. The poison in her side burned through her system. She could feel the beasts inside her, she simply couldn't call them.

Rough hands grabbed her black hair and pulled her to him. "Suck it whore, or I skin the pup while you watch."

Monique trembled with anger. If she submitted then all was lost, she would rather die than be this man's plaything.

"I would, but it's so small I can't find it." She barely spoke when he slapped her hard across the face. The world went red. Her eyes crossed and she had trouble seeing.

"I…"

Suddenly, Carver slammed into the man, his blood-soaked torso knocking him down. Brennan screamed and thrashed. The other wolves looked confused as blood pooled on the ground. Brennan clawed frantically at Carver's back as the big man pushed him hard to the ground. Monique got her footing, reached down to the barb, and with all her strength she pulled it out. The flesh around it tore with a sickening sound, she nearly blacked out from the pain, but the barb was out.

Carver punched Brennan several times, the scar faced wolf jerked his limbs feebly, pushing against his attacker. Then, suddenly, his limbs went limp, and a dying gurgle escaped his lips. Carver stood, bloody knife in hand. Monique looked back to the jail. She must have dropped it when she shifted into bear. Kirk trotted across the ground to sit beside her. The silence of the moment was only broken by the continual fire alarm. They all stood there and watched Brennan bleed out the last of his blood.

Finally, Carver tossed the knife on the corpse.

"He told you about a path, one that was easy, and full of reward. I tell you, no such path exists. Life is hard, the pack is hard, but it is also rewarding.

Throw down your weapons, swear fealty to me, and you can join my pack, and I will protect you. But, if for one moment I ever think you're against Kirk, or me… Monique."

She smiled. She didn't know what he wanted, but she knew what she did. She threw her head back and screamed. The scream turned to a roar has her body shifted into a giant polar bear.

*

Monique lay among the elk furs in the small warren that was their home. The mine shaft had many such warrens that the different couples called their own. This one was lined with faux fur rugs and pillows, with a draw string curtain over the door. Oddly enough, there wasn't anything from the cabin she wanted. They went back for the food she left, because that was always important, but everything else seemed like it belonged to another life.

She nuzzled Carver in the neck, her soft lips making little noises as she ran them down to his chest. Her tongue slipped out to circle his nipple. She moaned as he ran a hand down her side, tweaked her nipple, then followed the crease of her flat stomach to her pussy. His fingers slipped into the wet folds to stimulate her sensitive area. His fingers hooked inside of her and held her waist so she couldn't pull away. He smiled at her as she ground her hips into his hand. *Dammit, not this time.* He had a habit of making her cum first, of always making her cum first, and often. This time though, she wanted to win.

It was difficult to concentrate as her orgasm built. She ran her tongue down his stomach to the patch of hair above his cock. She slipped her mouth suddenly around the whole head and he froze. She took the opportunity to lift her legs and straddle his face so that her pussy hovered above his lips.

"Race you," she mumbled around a mouth full of cock.

CHAPTER NINE

Monique glided through the woods, a white streak of grace and speed. Her snow leopard self leaped from branch to tree, over rocks and streams, and through piles of leaves without disturbing neither birds nor mice. Finding Kirk was her focus. Her sensitive nose, combined with exceptional eyesight, let her follow his trail through the woods even as the sky turned from black, to gray, to pink.

Sounds drifted in the air that didn't belong in the forest. She held up. Her nose could tell her that the scents were fresh, but not how close. Now though, she could hear someone talking. She froze. The people weren't too far ahead of her. She needed to see them before she attacked. The trees faded to her right and grew stronger to her left. She followed the thicker bushes and trees. After a dozen yards, she spied an opening in the brush. Kirk, with barely a stitch of clothing on him, held Portia close to his chest. *He must be freezing. Even with his elevated heat...* She couldn't make out the words, but they stopped. Kirk sat Portia down, kissed her head, and then everything exploded. Nah grabbed him by his throat and lifted him up off the ground to push him against the tree.

Monique shifted as she moved. The delicate cat was replaced by the vicious bear. The woman didn't have time to scream as the massive paw came down on her head. Kirk kicked Nah in the stomach, then slammed her head first into the tree. Portia was in his arms a heartbeat after that. Then he ran.

Nah recovered from the tree, Monique roared at her. The woman backed off, stripping off her jacket and tossing her useless firearm to the side.

"You're one of us, why are you helping them?"

Monique paused, one of her massive paws hung in the air.

"You're not one of us... the stories are true. Time for you to meet a true shifter, not a pretender like yourself."

Nah threw her head back and screamed. It shifted to a roar along with her body. Skin melted and reformed into shaggy brown fur. A bear the size of a VW bug faced off with her where a woman had been seconds before.

The shock of seeing another bear kept Monique from stopping the first blow. Sharp, straight claws ripped through the sensitive flesh of her nose and face. She jumped back on her hind legs, then toppled forward to use her superior weight. Nah was ready for it. Being smaller and faster, the brown bear used her speed to the utmost advantage. She darted out of the way and sunk her teeth into Monique's haunches. The polar bear roared as pain shot up her back side.

The brown bear seemed to be everywhere. Biting teeth and slashing claws left a dozen red patches on her white fur. The wind shifted and a new scent caught Monique's attention. Nah was stalling her. She had help coming, and fast. Nah may have been a superior bear, but she wasn't fighting just another bear.

Her body ached as she shifted back to human, the wounds bled on her skin. Nah paused.

"You're a better fighter than me, but that's only the second time I've been a bear."

Monique turned and ran. She heard the bear grunt behind her as it pushed its mass after her. Monique focused on the wind as it rushed pass her face. Her muscles burned as she leaped into the air. Her white feathers spread out beside her. With a piercing scream, she was a hundred feet up.

Unfortunately, as a hawk, she had exceptional vision, but almost no sense of smell. She caught sight of Kirk, but no sign of who was coming to help Nah, though she was sure it was another bear. With an eye on Kirk, she drifted up another few hundred feet.

On the horizon, the cabin appeared. *I wondered why they were going up. Either she's really hurt or he's hoping there's someone there who can help.* Kirk was already halfway there; he would make it on foot before Nah could catch up with him. Monique's fight with her bought him enough time. With a flap of her wings, she sent herself into a dive that brought her to the cabin in a few seconds. The window sat open. She zipped in, catching her wing tip on the edge.

The cabin wasn't small. Two bedrooms, a common area and big fire pit, and a kitchen. She shifted to a human once inside. The pit burned with a bright flame. All the bedding was stacked against one wall along with the guest pillows.

Johan walked out of the kitchen, a bottle of beer in his hand. He stopped cold when his eyes found Monique's naked form. Her wounds were almost healed, and she was covered in a layer of mud and dirt. None of that hid her breath-taking beauty though. The bottle shattered when it hit the ground.

"Johan, thank god. Is the radio working?"

"Why are you naked?"

Monique looked down at her state of undress. Her clothes were long gone, left somewhere outside the resort.

"Listen, in a few seconds Kirk is coming through that door with a human girl. She's very important, and she's hurt. Is the radio working?"

It took him a second, but when she walked up to him and put her hand on his shoulders that snapped him out of his reverie.

"Yeah, it's fine. Uh, this way."

"Excellent, now here's what we need to do." She explained her plan to him, with each word she spoke his eyes widened.

"Are you serious?"

"As a heart attack."

CHAPTER TEN

Monique smiled. It was a good day. The store carried all the supplies they needed for the last three weeks at the resort, they wouldn't have to go out of pocket on a delivery and hope that it got there in time. If they had more time, she would order everything via the internet, but a colossal second half of the summer left them with little supplies to finish out the season. Monique finished paying and went outside. It would take the store a few minutes to gather everything and load it into her pick-up. The old Ford navigated the treacherous mountain roads like a goat, and she used it every time she came to town.

How often now, three, four times a year? It was a far cry from when she came to town only when her life depended on the supplies. The large glass window showed her who she was now, unrecognizable was the survivor of five years past. Monique's long black hair swung in an elegant braid over her left shoulder to rest on her breasts. She wore a loose, white blouse that highlighted the tops of her cleavage, and draped down over her stomach to come up shy of her slim jeans. The effect was contrasted by her creamy dark skin and long legs. After Katrina, she stopped dressing in any way that could be considered sexy; she stopped feeling, stopped thinking, only lived to survive. That woman didn't exist anymore.

Now Monique had other problems. She leaned up against the truck, her eyes wandering and unfocused at the memory of her and Carver's passion from the night before. Moisture blossomed between her legs, her heart pounded in her chest. More than anything, she wanted to fuck. Her skin tightened, nipples hardened as her body responded to her thoughts. She grabbed the handle of the truck to steady herself. Without realizing it, she slipped a hand between her legs and pushed. She moaned, her breath came in ragged chunks. *God what has he done to me? Ever since I changed, it's like I'm a nymph. The thought of him, or anyone else, and I'm dizzy!*

A hand touched her shoulder and snapped her out of her daze.

"You okay? You look like you could use some help," a young man, not more than twenty, asked her. She blinked a couple of times, removed her hand from her waistband, and turned around. Her cheeks blushed from the way they licked their lips. There were three of them. It wasn't their fault, Carver warned her this would happen, he reminded her whenever she went to town. Shifters put off pheromones that affected those around them. Powerful shifters, like herself, could control the emotions of people from a distance, and even force them to behave in a way they wouldn't otherwise act.

As soon as she turned around, the young man who spoke lunged at her. He slammed her up against the truck, his lips found hers and he forced his tongue in her mouth. She closed her eyes for just a moment. In no way did she want to be unfaithful to Carver, she loved him. The feelings that ran through her that moment weren't based on love, but a deep need to feel a cock between her legs. His hands pushed up her blouse, her hard nipples ready for attention.

No, no, no, this is as bad as when I acted only to survive. I'm not going to be a slave to my emotions. Slowly, as not to injure the man, she pushed him off her. A sigh escaped her lips at the thought of them taking her.

"I'm sorry, it's not your fault, but I can't."

His glossy eyes, muddled from her pheromones, shifted from excitement to anger. His grip on her tightened, he let a snarl out, and pushed back toward her. She would have none of it. His hand crumpled under hers as she bore down on him, twisting his wrist back over his forearm. He whimpered and his friends froze as she put him on his knees.

"I said no." She kicked him to the ground. Her steely eyes told the other two she was done. They dragged their friend away.

The store loaded up her truck. The thousand dollars' worth of supplies took up the whole bed. If anyone wondered why she sat in the cab, with the windows up, and the A/C at full blast, no one said anything.

Once loaded, she pointed the old pick-up out of town. It used to be a short drive to the edge, but that was before Monique, with Carver's money, bought the land around her uncle's cabin and turned it into a resort. The wolves were natural guides, it turned out. Hunters, naturalists, nature lovers, and those looking for an unusual spot to have a vacation, flocked to *Sienna Hills Resort and Spa.* The spa part was her idea. Their pack now numbered almost forty; fifteen of those were girl wolves. While they were wolves, they were also women; having the spa to run and work went a long way to their happiness. It also brought in female clients for the unattached wolves to prey on. While Carver kept a strict policy about how his male wolves treated women, they weren't prevented from sleeping with the human girls, as long as they didn't force them, or hurt them. His feelings on women's choice were adamant.

It worked though; the girls that mated within the pack were taken care of, those that stayed single, or at least available, were ever popular, and the single men got enough attention from visiting girls to satiate their lust. After the first year, word got out about 'the hunks' that worked there, and business boomed. She smiled at the thought; not that they would prostitute out anyone, but the male wolves who played the game loved it, the women who visited loved it, and everyone won. The town, along with the resort, grew. Once, only a few hundred people lived there. Now, Monique navigated three stop lights, and well over a mile of residential area before leaving the city limits.

The weather stayed nice and sunny for the drive home. The higher the road climbed into the mountains, the more attention it required. The pavement ended at the old Ranger station, it was only marked with a monument now, the new station—courtesy of a donation by Carver—stood a few miles higher up, on the other side of the ravine. She rolled her windows down for the last few miles; the smell of the forest, and the clean air of the mountains put a smile on her face.

*

"I swear to god, Johan, give me a reason not to tear your fucking throat out right now," roared Carver. His shoulders bulged and he heaved himself up from behind his desk. Johan shrunk before his rage.

"I can't help myself," he squeaked. "She's… every time I look at her, my heart aches." Genuine tears rolled down his cheeks, his skin flushed red with shame. Carver backed off his presence, his anger only a façade to get the truth from the man. If he were a would-be rapist, Carver would know. In this case though, his instincts told him different.

"Sit down, son." Carver pointed at the chair. He came around and sat one haunch on the immense oak desk.

"I see it now: you do love her, but what you have to understand is she doesn't love you back." Carver put a hand on Johan's shoulder. The man dissolved into sobs. Carver called him a man, but he was barely twenty-three. Most of the wolves, including Krystal, the object of his affection, were older and wiser. Johan came to them two winters before, half-starved, and desperate. Carver took him in, but trouble followed the young man. Carver would have to have words with Krystal; her willingness to fuck anyone wasn't an issue as long as she acted responsibly. Any half-blind idiot could see how much pain Johan felt with each beat of his heart; Carver even more so than most. His position as Alpha wasn't just ceremonious, it came with power and responsibility, something he took solemnly.

Since he met Monique, things changed. Almost immediately. He had always cared for their physical well-being, but now he cared for their mentality as well. The resort stood as a beacon of brilliance on her part. A place where they could mingle with humans on their own territory, as themselves, and not draw unwanted attention. At least, until now. He glanced at the envelope on his desk, the seal of the United States Senate emblazoned on the front.

"What do I do? What can I do?" Johan said.

Carver shook his head, grateful for the question; a hopeless man would look for blame without himself, Johan wanted to fix things.

"I think the first thing we need to do is get you away from her." He held up his hand to forestall any argument. "This isn't punishment, Johan, and you're not being banished." Johan's shoulder sunk with obvious relief.

"I don't want to hurt her, or anyone, Alpha, honest."

"I know, and if I thought you did, you would already be dead. No, Johan, this whole thing is unfortunate. You're a good worker, son: you show up on time, you've got great instincts. I think I can help you sort this out. You know about the hunting lodge we maintain in the winter?"

Johan nodded. Usually they left the lodge vacant during the winter. Last year, some poachers used it as a base, and left it vandalized. Short of hiring someone to live on the mountain in isolation for the winter, Carver didn't have many options. Until now.

"I want you to pack a good kit, make a list, and have Monique sign off on it." Johan blinked with confusion. "She knows more about survival on this mountain than any natural-born wolf ever will. Have her sign off on it, and the store will outfit you. I want that cabin ship-shape, make any repairs you need to, any improvements. too. I'll come up in the spring and inspect. Six months on your own will do you a world of good, especially knowing you have a home to come back to, deal?" They shook. Johan left the office with a spring in his step Carver hadn't seen since he met the man.

He completely lost track of time after Johan left. Paperwork, bills, complaints, booking problems, they were enough to overwhelm him. The resort brought in tremendous capital, especially since their overhead remained low. They did need to hire a few employees here and there, but not many. Most of the work could be carried out by the pack.

The letter on the side of the desk caught his attention again. He glanced at the clock. Monique would be back soon. He needed to tell her. As if on cue, the door opened. Framed in the setting sun of his office window, Monique paused to smile at him. His breath caught in his throat. A thin, white tank top clung to her melon sized breasts. Her hard nipples strained the fabric. His eyes roamed down to her bare, taught stomach, then to her white thong covered by a lacy garter belt. Stockings went down to her high-heeled shoes.

"If you don't fuck me right now, I'm going over to the bungalow and starting an orgy," she said, her voice thick with passion. Carver leaped over the table, pinned her against the wall, and pressed his body to hers.

"Don't make promises you can't keep," he breathed into her ear. Her hands unbuckled his pants as his pulled her wet thong aside.

"Who said I wouldn't?" Her voice sounded almost sincere. Carver luxuriated in the feel of her hands on his member as she guided it to her pussy. He pulled her top off, found one of her hard nipples, and grazed it with his teeth. Her hot snatch invited him in; he moaned with her tit in his mouth as the head of his cock penetrated her. She grunted, wrapped one leg around his waist, and opened herself to him.

"Fuck me hard, Carver," she moaned. He obliged. His cock slid a few inches into her. Then out, and back in. With each thrust he sunk deeper into her. She screamed when he got six inches in. Her body shuddered and her pussy clamped on him like a vice when he bottomed out at ten inches. Her eyes rolled up in her head as she screamed. Her orgasm shook her whole body. Carver grunted with her, his heart pounded as he slammed into her. Each thrust brought him immeasurable pleasure. More so though, he loved what it did for her. He clamped down on his own growing orgasm; he wanted her pleasure to last the night.

The sun sunk behind the western mountains to the sound of Monique's orgasms.

*

Monique awoke to light kisses on her face. *No, not kisses,* she brushed a cold snout away from her. "Kirk," she snarled playfully. The pup's ability to sneak into any room as quiet as a mouse continued to amaze her.

"Okay, boy, I'm up." He stopped his attempts at licking her and lay beside her. She responded by rubbing his ears. He wasn't really a pup any more, she mused. Not after five years. He wasn't quite full grown, but he wasn't a boy anymore either.

"Are you going to shift today, huh?"

His eyes met hers, and he didn't respond.

"Well, it's okay, when you're ready. Where's your dad?" The wolf looked to the door. The sound of a shower drifted from the closed bathroom. Monique stretched, letting the blanket fall down her curves. Her breasts ached from the mauling Carver gave them. She sighed at the sight of her clothes. Once they got going… She would need new lingerie. Kirk averted his gaze as she stood up. Somehow, it never occurred to her to cover up around him. Ever since she met the pup, that day on the mountain five years before, her life changed. More than her mental shift, or her ability as his guardian, but something she still didn't fully understand. She looked at her body in the mirror. Not for a second did she look thirty-one. More like twenty-one.

"I admire it too, probably as much as you," Carver said from the bathroom door.

She smiled at the compliment. Steam drifted into the room refreshing the perpetually dry air. Carver padded over to his son, ran a hand through his thick mane. "Is today the day, boy?" The wolf gave him the same blank stare.

"He will when he's ready," Monique said as she slipped on her yoga pants. The stretchy fabric only enhanced her sex-appeal. She followed it up with a long tank top, a sports bra, and another tank top.

"I always wondered how you keep those monsters in check when you run."

"You get to wear pants around yours, I have no such luck, so layers it is." She slipped on her shoes, grabbed her sunglasses, and headed for the door.

"Monique, there's something we need to talk about." She didn't like the sound in his voice. She closed the door, and waited.

"We're getting a visitor. You know the Fish and Wildlife people have been up here all summer 'evaluating us'?"

Monique suppressed a shiver. Since the beginning of spring, she'd been dealing with mid-level bureaucrats concerned about a forest they never even stepped foot in. She couldn't tell them that the wolves were better equipped to preserve the balance of nature than some paper pusher in D.C.

"What now?" she said with exasperation.

"A US Senator is visiting us tomorrow. His name is Paul Rogers; have you heard of him?"

The name sounded familiar to her, but she couldn't place it. "Is he the senator from Vermont?" she guessed.

"No, Montana. He's the head of the Wildlife preserve committee, and they are preparing a brief for the President that would name this part of Vermont a National Monument."

Monique's fist clenched involuntary. *That's ridiculous.* If they made the area a monument, Carver would have to close up shop. No resort, no buildings, they could still act as guides but they couldn't live there. The wolves would of course, but Monique couldn't shift into a wolf. And she couldn't spend a long time in any of her three forms. Not like the wolves who could live out their lives in one form or the other. She couldn't go back to living in a cave either. Half the reason they bought the resort was to try and live a normal life.

"Do you think he'll do it?"

"There's more, and you're not going to like it." He rubbed his face. "He's a wolf, and not just any, he heads up the North American council. He's the single most powerful Alpha in the country."

She sighed. *Of course.* They just didn't interact with other packs. The nearest one was in the Appalachians three hundred miles away. The only new wolves Monique saw were the occasional lone wolves that came looking for a place to call home.

"What's this mean for us? Will he be favorable to us? Or will he want your power?"

"I would like to think, in a perfect world," Carver said, "that he would do what's best for the land. But with Kirk, and you, in the equation, I just don't know." Monique sat next to him, leaned into his shoulder, rubbed his back, and squeezed.

"We don't talk much about Kirk. What is he?" It was something Monique always wanted to ask, but the time never felt right.

"Honestly, he may be nothing more than a normal wolf." She raised an eyebrow at that. "There's an old legend, old even for my people, that a single wolf will be born once every thousand years, to defend his people, to lead them to greatness. It's been a long time since that's happened. The last one, a man of great strength and charisma, united Europe in a way no person ever had. Part of his power was his guardian. A ferocious creature capable of great violence."

Monique giggled, "I guess I'm pretty ferocious." She gently punched him in the ribs.

"Well, like I said, it's just a legend. Kirk's birth fell on the full moon, and he was born as a wolf, neither of those events are unusual. His mother though, my darling Sienna, she was convinced that the signs were all in place. It fell on the seventh full moon of the year, which also happened to be the seventh super moon of the year. It wasn't until they killed her that I believed her."

Monique sensed the sorrow in him, his longing for his dead wife, and even a little guilt from his pairing with her.

"She would be proud of you. Look how you've taken care of your pack, of your son. She would be proud," she whispered to him. Carver squeezed her leg.

CHAPTER ELEVEN

He wasn't ready. Six months alone, up in the mountains, and he had to leave her behind. But he trusted Carver, trusted his Alpha's instincts. His little room in the bungalow, with its bare shelves, and empty drawers, was his home. Before he joined Carver's pack, he had nothing. Now, he at least had hope. He slung his pack over his shoulder, gave the room one last look, and closed the door behind him. List in hand, he left to find Monique.

She wasn't too hard to find, for a human she worked as hard as any wolf. If it wasn't overseeing the chef to make sure the staff and guests ate on time, it was on the grounds looking for things to improve, or in the buildings inspecting them for cleanliness.

The staff admired her, and they were afraid of her. Johan wasn't sure why they skirted around her in the hall, or avoided looking directly at her when she spoke. The male wolves whispered about her, about her obvious prowess, and how she killed several invading wolves years back. The girls seemed less impressed, and more jealous than anything. Krystal never mentioned her. But then, he barely spoke to her. Oh, how he wished he could make her see that his love for her was real, they she could be satisfied with him. *No. You can't, Carver's right, you need to get some distance.*

He found Monique at the pro shop; she walked through each aisle, checking each piece of ammo, firearm, and hunting equipment. Her black hair fell in waves down her back, contrasting with her white tank top. Even though she dressed in layers, the outline of her body had an immediate effect on him. He felt his member stir to life, and his face flushed with heat. He coughed politely to let her know he was there.

"Yes?" she said without looking up from her clipboard.

"Carver sent me to have you check off my list. I'm going up to watch the cabin for the winter."

She turned to him, her green eyes lit up on contact with his face. He couldn't help but smile.

"Excellent, it was such a disappointment to have it vandalized, and honestly, who's going to want to spend the winter up there that doesn't already live here? Thank you so much." Her honesty and sincerity struck Johan, he found himself instantly liking her.

"Carver thinks it's a good idea.," he said lamely. Not sure how to respond, he stood there, playing with an item on the shelf.

"The list?"

"Right!" He fumbled in his pocket for the paper. She took it from his shaking hand with a strange look. He wiped his brow as she scanned the list. His mouth went dry. Johan stumbled over to the counter to get away from her. *What's wrong with me? That's the Alpha's girl, and she's not even a shifter.* He grabbed a bottle of water from the counter and downed it in one go. From the corner of his eye, he watched her scan the list. Her lips pouted as she thought, the skin over her brow furrowed. She placed a hand on her curvy hips and jutted it out to the side. Johan's heart threatened to break out of his chest. He clenched his fist around the water.

"Everything looks good. I would suggest you take more ammo than you think you need, though, you never know." She held the paper out to him, her head cocked sideways with a little smile.

"Thanks." He snatched the paper and tried not to run out of the store. He made it to the bathroom, splashed cold water on his face, and took in a few deep breaths.

*

Monique leaned against the old pickup she used to get to town. Kirk sat on his haunches at her side; his head reached to her side now and she absently rubbed his ears with one hand. They'd been waiting an hour for the senator's arrival. All the staff that could be excused from duties waited with them, twenty-five in total, all wolves. The humans were left on their jobs; while a visiting senator ranked as a big deal, the wolf politics of the situation demanded more from the pack.

Carver smiled at her from across the drive. His suit and tie looked out of place to her. He belonged in something far more casual. *Or nothing at all.* Visions of him on his knees in front of her colored her cheeks. *Whoa girl, it's not like we didn't have sex an hour ago. What is wrong with me? Four years we've been together, and yeah we have a lot of sex but this...* Until a few days ago, Monique thought she was just being horny. Now, though, she wondered if there wasn't something else going on. Her own body had strange powers and presented itself as a bit of a mystery. She couldn't ask anyone how a guardian's body worked, since no one lived who could answer the question. Not only that, she had the wolves to worry about. Carver told her on a number of occasions that their pheromones were dangerous. She blushed at her indiscretion in town.

Kirk's ears picked up, his whole body stiffened.

"You okay?" she asked as she knelt beside him. He growled, and ran. *He's not a baby anymore, wolves mature much faster than people. The fact that's he's never changed means he's probably at least a teenager in there.*

Still, it struck her as odd as she watched him high tail it to the resort. Her thoughts were interrupted by the sound of gears changing and tires on gravel. She stood back up, walked over to Carver, and took his hand in hers. They squeezed each other for support.

The first truck screamed government with its black paint and tinted windows. All four doors opened at once and men in black suits got out and proceeded to secure the area. The passenger side revealed an Asian women with sharp features and short black hair. She snarled as she walked around the front of the truck.

"Collins, get that building over there checked out. Roberts, down to the forest line," she barked as she approached Carver and Monique.

"Special Agent Nah, I'm the head of the senator's security detail."

"Carver…," he started to say when she cut him off.

"That building is new." She pointed to the western bungalow.

Monique spoke up, not liking her tone, or the way she spoke to Carver. "Define new? We put it in last year. It's for our year-round staff," she said defensively. The women brought out her edge, she had to keep herself from growling.

"It's not on our photos or your blueprints. My people are going to have to search it." She turned to yell something at her agents. Carver put a hand on Monique's arm to stop her from arguing.

"Our people live there," she whispered to Carver.

"I know, but we need this to go off without a hitch. Just let them do their job; it'll be okay."

Monique let out a sigh. She wasn't used to people telling her what to do.

The agent walked away without a word, engrossed in her work. Monique couldn't tell if she was a wolf or not. Nothing about her screamed it, but she couldn't always tell. Carver could, but not her. Now wasn't the time to ask, though.

A second, identical SUV followed up the road. It came to a stop a hundred feet behind the first, the large engine under the hood idled for a moment before shutting off. Agent Nah led a small team down to meet it. Carver, unsure what to do, followed with Monique in tow.

A hand slid itself into hers and startled her. A young man of seventeen, with eyes as gray as an overcast sky, and wearing clothes that didn't fit, walked beside her. Her breath caught sharply when she realized who it was.

"Hi, Mom, uh, did I do this right?" Kirk asked. His clothes were all from the lodge store, a sweatshirt, yoga pants, and a pair of sandals. While too big, they all were on correctly.

"Kirk?" Carver whispered with awe in his voice. "My boy," he said.

"Hi, Dad. I'll explain later," he said to answer the obvious question Monique had on her mind.

The senator exited the car. He was a tall man with a weather-beaten face, and at least a day's stubble. He pulled it off well, looking as if he stepped out of the cover of 'Outdoor' magazine. His suit fit him in all the right ways, and he moved with the grace of a lion. *No,* Monique corrected herself, *a wolf.* Her heart fluttered, sweat gathered on her brow, and her thighs trembled. *Not now. God, not now.*

Behind the senator, a young woman came into view. Long blond hair framed a heart shaped face. Her blue eyes peaked out behind half closed lids. Monique, in her haze, could feel Kirk's hand grip her tight, and suddenly she realized why he chose now to shift.

CHAPTER 12

After a brief conversation with his security detail, the senator came over to meet them. Monique kept an eye on Agent Nah as she led a team to the employee's bungalow. She still didn't like them searching the place. Much of her fear, she admitted, could be down to her inherent distrust of the government after Hurricane Katrina. After all, the city, state, and even the federal government abandoned the city long before they told the people to evacuate. She squelched that line of thinking, though. It usually led to a sad place, and right now she needed her thoughts straight. Her body was playing tricks on her enough.

The sun shined through a clear sky, and the temperature sat at a balmy seventy-five. Perfect for September, and for the resort. The senator's trip couldn't have been planned for a better time.

With Carver in one hand, and Kirk in the other, Monique waited for him to approach. He rose a head taller than everyone around him, and from his build she could tell he used it to his advantage. Carver, while broad and six feet, fell five inches short of the senator.

"Senator Rogers, may I introduce Monique? She pretty much runs the place, and our son, Kirk." Monique heard Carver speaking, but couldn't take her eyes of the senator. His blue eyes, the same shade as his daughter's enthralled her, almost calling to her.

"Carver, it's good to see you again, and I'm glad to hear of your success; the place looks great," the big man said as he shook hands, first with Carver, then he held out his hand to Monique. She stared at it dumbly, like it was a snake. Carver coughed politely. Monique shook herself and reached out. The air snapped between them when their hands touched. He didn't seem to notice, but Monique had to bite her bottom lip to keep from calling out.

Kirk reached out lamely, not having ever shaken a hand before. He dropped his after a few seconds. Senator Rogers turned to wave his daughter over. Monique took a step back and leaned against the truck the second he looked away.

"Are you okay?" whispered Carver. She looked at him, his brown eyes, soft features, her heart swelled with love. How then, could she be vibrating with the desire to pull this man she just met into an embrace? All she could muster to answer Carver was a blank stare.

"This is my daughter, Portia; she's supposed to be with her mom this weekend, but things didn't work out."

"That's his polite way of saying my mom took off with her latest guy for the weekend and forgot about me," Portia said.

Kirk held his hand out to her. Monique wiped her brow with her forearm, took a deep breath, and got herself under control. Despite her feelings, she had to see this through, at least until she could be alone. When Kirk's hand touched Portia's she felt the spark all over again. Only the fact that she still leaned against the truck kept her from falling over.

"Carver, I need to lay down."

"Of course, Senator, please come with me, I'll give you the tour. Will Portia be joining us?"

Monique managed to look up and she saw in Kirk's face a little of what she felt. He and Portia held hands, frozen in mid-shake, staring at each other.

"Portia?"

The blond girl blushed, quickly pulled her hand away, and looked at her dad.

"Sorry, uh, yeah sure… Could Kirk maybe show me around? There's a pool right? I would love a swim," she said.

Carver looked to the senator, who nodded, then back to his son. "Go ahead, be back in time for dinner."

Monique put her arm around Carver's waist and let him help her walk. She needed to lay down and figure out what was going on before it drove her insane.

*

If it wasn't for her loser mom, she wouldn't have had to come to this place. Her dad was constantly jetting off to some part of the country, either for fund raisers or business. Normally, she would've stayed home, but when she found out her mom's wasn't an option, well, a resort in the mountains sounded better than her room and bodyguard baby sitters. Now, with Kirk at her side, she didn't think things were so bad.

Her skin itched in a way it never had. She looked at him and her mouth watered, her stomach ached, she trembled trying to say his name. That wasn't like her. She didn't have nerves, and she certainly didn't have trouble talking to boys. Especially not ones with shaggy brown hair and eyes like an overcast sky. And his lips, she blushed thinking about what she would like those lips to do to her... *What is wrong with you? Stop it!*

A warmth in her hand made her realize that she had inadvertently reached out to hold his hand as they walked around behind the resort. When had she done that?

"Kirk, I don't feel like swimming in a pool, is there somewhere else we can go?" she asked him.

Kirk cast his gaze at her for a moment, his features flickered insecurely.

"There's a hot springs not too far away, the staff keeps it for themselves. This time of day it should be all ours," he said.

"Perfect, let's go there," Portia said with a smile. When he turned to pull her to the woods, she wiped one hand across her face.

He led her behind the resort, up a small trail that disappeared into the woods. The birch trees mingled with the evergreens giving the forest an eerie dark and light look. The trail evened out and from her vantage point she could see the whole resort. She stopped to look at it; even at seventeen, she could appreciate the beauty of it. The main building sat nestled up to the cliff they just climbed, behind it was the pool and jacuzzi. The front of the place looked over its main grounds, the bungalow her dad's people were freaked out about, the storage room, and a shed.

On the other side was the basketball court, and the indoor shooting range. The whole place seemed to grow right out of the mountain, no artificial grass, or garish colors.

"Your people really make this place look like it belongs," she said as they continued down the trail.

"Uh, my people?"

"You know, wolves, you're a wolf right?"

He stopped short, peering at her. She smiled back. Of course she knew, her dad was one, and she could be one someday if she wanted. He was careful to keep her out of pack business, but she was smart, and clever, there wasn't a whole lot he could hide from her.

"You know about us?" Kirk asked.

She couldn't tell if it was a smile or a frown, and that bothered her. Reading people, especially boys, came second nature to her. This one though, she couldn't see anything about him.

"It's not a big secret; my father's an Alpha, of course I know. Come on, I'm dying to get out of these clothes," she said as she pushed past him. *That ought to get him thinking!* She followed him up the trail and around the ridge that took them out of sight of the resort. They passed a sign warning hikers that that the area was unstable and full of unexplored caves.

"Is it safe?" she asked. The boy just nodded to her. He was infuriatingly silent. She was used to boys prattling on, trying to impress her with knowledge or feats of strength. This one, this Kirk, seemed content to let her talk. And she was. She barely even knew what she said for the twenty minutes they walked through the forest. Suddenly he stopped, lifted his finger to her lips shushing her.

Anger flared through her at the presumption of being quieted. Before she could respond though, she heard it. A trickle of water against rocks.

"We're almost there, if we're quiet we might catch a deer drinking." He crouched down and moved slowly down the trail. Mimicking him, her anger forgotten, she followed. The dirt trail was well worn from boots and shoes traversing it. The sides were slightly muddy, but mostly it was a dry path. Kirk pushed a bush aside and Portia saw the hot springs. It wasn't as large as the pool, perhaps twenty feet across, but it was beautiful. Black lava rock encircled the edges, the bushes were cleared back a few feet to allow room to relax on the bank. Heat shimmered on the surface of the mildly bubbling water. A small stream fed in from the north side, and beside the stream, a fawn dipped down to drink the water. It wasn't like she'd never seen a deer before, but not this close.

Kirk moved like a shadow, his feet not making a sound as he stepped over the brook. The deer only flinched when he placed his hand between its ears and gently rubbed. It bleated in happiness.

Portia couldn't take her eyes off him. A smile spread on her face, and warmth flowed through her. She liked him. Not consciously, but she liked him more than any boy she'd met yet. He looked up to her. Blood rushed to her cheeks and she flushed with heat down to her toes. He smiled at her, a genuine smile that touched his gray eyes. She slipped her hands across her waist, grabbed the hem of her shirt, and pulled it off in one swift motion. She grinned at

Kirk's expression. Her shoes and jeans followed the shirt into a pile, leaving her clad only in her bra and thong.

"I can soak in here, right?" she asked with a confidence she didn't feel. The hot water rolled over her calves as she slowly sunk beneath the water. Her feet didn't touch the bottom. She bobbed gently, the tops of her breasts above the surface.

"Come in; you know you want to," she said with a wink.

CHAPTER 13

After they dropped Monique off in her room, Carver led the senator to the main hall. Paul dismissed his security personnel to get lunch at the restaurant and relax on the grounds. Agent Nah stayed with him, but at a respectful distance. Carver wasn't sure what to think of the man. Part of him wanted to like the older wolf. He had a grizzled complexion, a touch of gray hair, and steely blue eyes like his daughter. They were both Alphas, though, and that presented problems. He could smell Paul's attraction to Monique, and worse, he could sense her reciprocation. He didn't think for one minute she would ever cheat on him, but things were different for the wolves. Sometimes attraction was more than just a physical desire.

The two walked through the main hall, Carver taking the opportunity to assess the man and show off all of their hard work. The resort's interior was decorated with hardwood—oak and cherry. The walls were panelled and carved with images of wildlife. Spaced equally in the hall were hunting trophies, photographs, and even a few interior trees. There was something for everyone. The main hall, an elaborate room that could act as a gathering point for new guests, reception for events, or to give speeches, was every bit as ornate as the rest of the resort. Massive twin skylights let in natural light, and allowed a gorgeous view of the sky. Picture windows set in the second floor and angled slightly in, gave snapshots of the distant peaks.

"You've got a beautiful place here Carver, I can see why some people are upset," he said in his deep voice.

Carver bristled. "I'm not sure why anyone would be upset; we keep to ourselves up here, were not expanding our territory, and we certainly aren't hurting anyone, Senator."

The senator smiled. "Please call me Paul. It's going to be a long weekend if we go by official titles."

Carver nodded. "Paul it is."

"I'm not the enemy here Carver, quite the opposite. I want to help. I think what you've done up here is a fine bit of work."

Carver could sense the 'but' coming. So far, he remained quiet to evaluate which side of the fence

Paul fell on. He badly wanted the man to be an ally, at the same time he stifled his resentment that Monique seemed to have feelings for him, even if they weren't hers to control.

"I appreciate that, Paul, I do, we've worked hard, Monique has worked hard, to make it a good place for the pack. But I think we both know the Alphas aren't upset about a resort... Senator." While Carver talked, he watched the man's eyes. When he mentioned Monique's name, Paul's pupils dilated. *So it's not just her. Dammit, this complicates things.*

"You're as clever as I've been told, okay then. It's about your son. Is he the one?"

Carver could lie, the thought crossed through his mind, but any wolf would know that Monique wasn't one of them, and the reports of her shifting were too well known for him to hide. In the end, he took a chance.

"I think so, I can't be sure, no one can, but yes I think so." He couldn't stop himself from holding his breath. People would kill to control Kirk, or at least think that they controlled him. Carver hoped that the senator wasn't one of them.

His shoulders slumped, and he blinked his eyes a few times. "I'm in a precarious position, Carver. The council thinks that if your son is the one, then we should take possession of him. Obviously," he held up his hand, "as a father myself, I'm against that. But I'm not the end-all-be-all of the world at the end of the day, I'm one of six."

Carver nodded. Anxiety raced through him, not just about the thought of losing his son, but if anyone tried to take him... Monique could be hurt.

"He's already chosen his guardian. If anyone tries to take him against his will, I'm not sure you could stop her. She's... fierce." Carver wanted to say more, but his instincts told him to hold back.

"Is it Monique? Is that why she's... with you?" He seemed to be asking more than just if she worked here.

"Yes, she's with me. Kirk chose her, and I love her. Is that a problem?" He tried to keep the edge out of his voice, but from the way Paul tightened his jaw, he could tell that he failed

The two walked in silence. Carver led him up the staircase to the outdoor dining area. Unlit lanterns framed the area. It was one of Carver's favorite places at night.

"I didn't know, I want you to know that. I respect you, and I honor your pack, but if she chooses me…"

It was an old tale. The pheromones of a wolf were unpredictable. Sometimes they were just one-sided, usually with humans. The human would fall instantly and wildly in love with whomever triggered them. Other times it was a two-way street. The problem for Carver and Monique was that they didn't fall in love because of his pheromones, there wasn't anything keeping her from being attracted to another wolf. She loved him, but he knew the draw of the wolf's charm. It's what brought him and Sienna together. Resisting it was an exercise in futility.

Carver caught a whiff of Kirk's new scent, the smell of human almost hid the wolf. He also smelled something else, he smiled.

"Your daughter's back," he said to Paul as he turned to walk away. "Things are happening at a fast pace, Paul, change is always painful and messy, we don't have to make it worse by acting hastily," Carver finished as he walked out. He had nothing else to say to the senator.

CHAPTER 14

Monique sighed into the mirror. She desperately tried to picture Carver kissing her. His lips on her neck, traveling down her collarbone. Each time, though, it turned into Paul. Lifting her up with his strong arms, his hard cock pushing against her.

No, no, no!

She took a deep breath and hissed it out through her teeth. Her heart was with Carver, but her body and mind seemed desperate for the man she just met. *How?* If she could just clear her head for a minute, for one second not be quivering between her thighs and desperate to be fucked, she could answer the question. Her hands squeezed the edge of her vanity as her breath came in gulps.

Her thighs quivered, she could feel the warmth of her nectar seeping down her legs.

"Hello," a voice said from her door. Had she missed someone knocking? With a surge of will power, she pushed herself up and went to the door. Paul stood on the other side. His casual shirt did little to hide his ripped physique. He opened his mouth to speak, but froze. His lips touched her before either realized what was happening. The door closed behind them and he pushed her up against the wall. Monique's soft skirt and white top were appropriate for sleeping, but so thin as to hide nothing. Her skin lit on fire as he ran his hand up her leg. Her mouth parted in a moan. He savagely attacked her lips, his hot tongue invaded her mouth. Monique's stomach tightened, her thighs shook as her orgasm built. *Oh god, I'm cumming.* His hands slipped under her shirt, callous fingers brushed her hard nipples. Bolts of lightning fired from her tits and she screamed into his mouth. She writhed against him, her hands found his pants and pulled the zipper down.

He pulled her skirt up to her waist. Monique broke her mouth away for his for a second to look down and pull his fly open. His massive cock sprang loose and pushed against her pussy. She guided the tip against her slit.

"Oh god, fuck me, do it now!"

He grunted as he slid the head of his dick into her. Monique clawed at his back.

She screamed as she fell over backward. The room was empty. Monique lay on the floor for a few minutes, desperate to collect her thoughts. She couldn't do this, she couldn't think. Carver told her about pheromones, but she never imagined they would be like this. What she needed was to get as far away from that man as she could. But she couldn't leave Kirk. The cabin on the north face, the one they sent the kid to for the winter... she could go there.

Monique leaped up and began packing. There was no time to lose. If she stayed she *would* cheat on Carver, and that wasn't something she wanted to take a chance with. A knock on the door interrupted her. She took a deep breath praying it wasn't Paul.

"Come in," she said from behind her bed.

"Mom, can I ask you something?" It was Kirk, his human form looked like the definition of a teenager. Shaggy brown hair, hands in his pockets, and clothes one size too big. It hid the taut young man underneath it. Like all wolves, Kirk's physique matched that of a professional athlete, in his case, he looked like a runner.

"Sure, baby, it's good to see you made the switch. If I had to guess, it's because of a certain blonde, isn't it?" she asked.

Kirk blushed as he shut the door behind him. He sat in the corner chair, slumped down with his legs stretched out.

"I didn't think it would be this hard, you know? I understood everything about life for a long time now. Growing up as a wolf has its advantages but… god, Mom, I can't breathe when I'm around her."

Monique smiled at him. Her heart beat with joy and love for her adopted son. Each time he called her 'Mom' made her want to leap for joy. She slipped on a pair of cargo pants under her long skirt then discarded the skirt. Next she pulled a turtle neck sweater over her head.

"You going on a trip?" Kirk asked.

"Listen honey, I say go where your heart is. From my experience, your wolf instincts know what's best for you," she said while she pulled on her hiking boots.

"Mom, you can't leave, this guy Paul is out of Dad's league, he needs you to help him."

At the mention of his name, her cheeks burned red. She turned away from her son, but there was no hiding her emotions from a wolf. It was only a matter of time until Carver figured it out.

"Oh… Mom… What are you going to do?"

"Obviously, I'm running. I'm not a wolf, Kirk, how long can I resist?"

Kirk ran his hands through his hair. She could see the interplay on his face. He was thinking about it, scanning through his knowledge of wolf behavior, and she could see him come to the same conclusion.

"A day, maybe two." He sighed.

"I've seen it happen a dozen times here at the resort. Men, women, they come up here, and they're lonely, they meet one of our pack, and…" She slapped her hands together. "I just thought if you were already in love, it would protect you," she said. She sniffed. Crying wouldn't help her, but she felt it coming on. Kirk put his arm around her and squeezed.

"This is my fault, I'm so sorry."

Monique smiled and ran her hands through his hair. He was a little taller than her now, which made it weird for him to stand next to her. She wasn't exactly short.

"You didn't choose this, and neither did I. None of that changes anything regardless. I have to go."

"You have to stay until tomorrow, Mom. By then, things will calm down and Paul will be on our side," he said.

Monique held him out to arm's length. She studied his face, trying to figure out what was going on behind his gray eyes.

"How can you be sure? And how do I fight this?"

"Well, let's just say things have a way of working themselves out. Trust me, after tomorrow you can still leave, but you may not have to."

*

Portia had her own room, which pleased her. The last thing she needed was her father's advice on what to wear for dinner. The bad news, for her, was that she hadn't planned for a nice weekend. The sexiest thing she brought were her under garments, and she couldn't exactly go to dinner with the entire pack wearing a red satin bra and a black thong. Her jeans were too casual, her shirts too frumpy; she tossed her suitcase against the wall. The mirror in the corner mocked her. At five-foot-nine she was considered tall, with a taut stomach from her daily swimming, and large breasts that came naturally; she was a knock out, and she knew it. But without the right clothes…

Kirk's mom! She wasn't exactly the same height as Portia, but close enough, surely she could spare something. She grabbed her robe, threw it on around her, and charged out the door. Her determination erased her uncertainty of not knowing where to go. After a few minutes of knocking on people's doors, she found the right one.

Kirk opened the door. Portia's heart nearly exploded as it beat in her ears. Everything went fuzzy and indistinct.

"Kirk, who is it?" Monique's voice came from the room beyond.

"It's Portia," he said, his own voice breaking in mid-sentence.

It cleared her head. She broke a smile, he returned it. They sat there smiling awkwardly at each other for a few seconds before Monique opened the door the rest of the way.

"Go," the older black woman said to her son, "get ready for dinner."

Portia unconsciously pushed against him as he brushed past her. She bit her lip to suppress a little cry. When she looked back to the door, Monique stood there staring at her.

"I see," she said to her.

"It's not what you think." Portia started to defend herself.

Monique held up her hands. "Stop, I'm fully in favor of you two, now why are you here? In a bath robe no less?"

Portia looked down, her mind catching up with her. *Kirk saw me in a robe...* Her hands flew to her face, she wore no makeup. Tears welled up in her eyes. Her hair wasn't done either.

Suddenly she was sobbing, and pointing, trying to make Monique understand the monumental catastrophe her life had just undergone. The woman put her hands on her shoulders and guided her in.

"It's okay, honey, he was too startled to see you, trust me."

*

The main hall was unrecognizable. Converted to a dining room by the staff, the tables were covered in silky cloth and artfully carved wooden chairs. For this dinner, Carver brought in a catering company (approved by the body guards) so that his pack could enjoy the special occasion. The sweet scent of roasted pork filled the hall. An entire wild boar lay slow roasting over a spit in the middle. A long buffet table ran the length, covered in meat, cheeses of all flavors, and fresh fruits and vegetables fried in olive oil. At the head of the table sat Carver, to his right, Monique. Opposite her sat the guest of honor, Paul, to his left was Portia, opposite Kirk.

Monique let out a quiet sigh as Carver stood to give a short speech. He had a gift for speaking, but she couldn't focus on it. Helping Portia get ready took her mind off her own problems, and she had to admit, it was fun having some girl time with her. Portia's natural good looks made it easy. Monique put her hair in an empire braid, dressed her in a blue, backless dress that never looked good on Monique, but it looked like it belonged on Portia. The soft swell of her breasts filled out the front, while giving her a hint of womanhood. The leggy blonde did the rest with her deft touch at makeup. She wore a dark red lipstick with just a hint of eye shadow, and finished off by splashing her face with a touch of glitter.

When every man in the room's mouth dropped open, Monique considered her a success. Her own dress was far more modest, and classically black, which wasn't what she normally wore. But she was trying to downplay herself, and let Portia be the center of attention. She briefly considered not even coming, but with such an effort put forward by Carver, she had to.

Applause brought her attention back to the present. Paul's blue eyes gazed at her from across the table. She blushed and looked away. Desperate for her hands to do something, she grabbed her champagne and took a long pull.

"I'd like to thank the senator for taking the time to review our home, and I hope he finds it in his heart to vote against taking it away from us!" More applause. Monique lifted her glass with everyone else, but it was empty.

One of the servers quietly made his way to her and refilled it.

The dining room filled with the quiet roar of conversation. Monique sipped her champagne, and tried to focus on anything but Paul. Carver's hand touched her thigh and she sighed. He was conversing with one of the senator's aides, but his fingers made small circles on her thigh. Inch by inch he pulled the hem of her dress up until his fingers touched naked skin.

"What are you doing?" she whispered into his ear.

"Distracting you, and reminding you," he said back.

He knows? Of course he knows, he can smell me. God what must he think?

"Monique, your husband tells me you're quite the outdoors woman, how did that come to be?"

She turned her head to Carver, her mouth open to answer and the words came out before she could stop them. "He's not my husband." She didn't mean it that way, they hadn't formally gotten married, or even talked about it. The bond they shared seemed stronger than that.

The smirk on Paul's face sent heat to hers. The temperature in the room shot up sharply. She downed her drink and held it out for another one. Carver's hand disappeared from her thigh, and he turned slightly away from her. She shot Paul a glare. He tipped his glass to her in return.

***

Portia glared at her father. She wasn't the most observant person but she could tell Monique and Carver were in love, why was her father digging at her like that? *Well, if he doesn't like him, he's going to hate me dating his son.* The delicious thought made her lips split into a slow smile. She ran one hand down the side of her dress, accentuating the swell of her breasts, her heart raced as Kirk's eyes followed her every move. She could look at him forever.

She took a drink of the apple juice, she wasn't allowed wine, and smiled at Monique. The woman smiled back, somewhat haggardly. *She doesn't look like she's having a good time.* Portia picked up her glass and spilled it on her dress. The juice soaked right through rendering the material somewhat translucent. Kirk gagged on his food as her nipples became crystal clear.

"Oh dear," she said with an exaggerated tone, "look what I've done. Daddy, I'm afraid I have to go change."

Paul didn't take his eyes of Monique when he waved to her in response.

"Monique, would you help me?"

"Of course, dear."

"Now, I don't think..." her dad said as he turned to look at her. His face immediately burned red as he glimpsed his daughters navel. "Yes of course, go make yourself decent," he muttered. Portia winked to Kirk as Monique held her arm to walk her out.

Once they were outside she whispered to her, "I'm sorry my dad is being such an ass. He has this way with women, and... well..." Portia let it trail off.

"It's not your fault, and to be honest, it's not entirely his either."

"My mom didn't seem to think that, it's why she left him. He always seemed to have a girl on the side, commitment be dammed." Portia loved her dad, but there were things about him that drove her crazy.

"Have you ever heard the story of the scorpion and the fox?" Monique asked her as they made their way outside. It was very cold in the mountains and her wet dress instantly flattened against her chest. The sudden cold material made her gasp for breath.

"Wow, cold. No, I haven't heard of it."

Monique hurried them to the second floor of residence. One inside the room, she turned up the heat while Portia stripped out of her dress.

"Once upon a time," she smiled at the girl, "a scorpion was trying to cross a river. He couldn't swim, and there was no spot to cross. Along came a fox," she continued, helping Portia out of her dress and giving her a towel to dry off, "and the scorpion asked him if he could ride across on his back."

"Well, that's just dumb, the scorpion would sting him," Portia interjected. From Monique's smile she gathered she guessed the ending.

"Wanting to help, the fox agreed. On the condition that the scorpion promised not to sting him. The scorpion agreed."

Dried off, Portia pulled on a thin pink sweater.

"The scorpion climbed on the fox's back and they swam across. Halfway there, the scorpion stung him. As the fox started to drown he asked, 'Why did you do it? Now we'll both die!' The scorpion responded, 'It's my nature.'"

Portia pondered it for a moment. "You're saying my dad can't help being a misogynistic asshole?"

Monique laughed. "Well, maybe he can, but it's his nature. He's a wolf, he hunts, he dominates, and there are women," she couldn't help but blush, "who find that irresistible."

CHAPTER 15

The rest of the dinner passed by in a blur after Portia left. The food on Kirk's plate tasted bland, the drink like water. In his mind, he pictured Portia next to him, smiling, laughing, eyes begging him to come to her. It was all he could do to not run away right that instant.

"What do you think of the use of the land?"

His father's voice drifted across the table. A moment of silence followed and he realized both men were looking at him. It was an old argument, and he picked up on most of it. There were groups who felt that people had no business being in the mountains, and there were groups who wanted to exploit the mountains.

"Animals and trees are a renewable resource if the caretakers are responsible about how they handle them. Our guides direct hunters so that they don't take strong mothers or endanger the predators or grazers. We work hard alongside the forest service to make sure we keep our numbers in check. While nature can certainly balance herself, we feel that we're helping the local wildlife stay vibrant and energetic. Considering the number of elk on the mountain stands at over two hundred where it was less than a hundred before, I'd say were doing a good job." He took a long pull from his apple juice after he spoke. He looked to the door in hopes that Portia was back, but there was still no sign of her.

Paul coughed, then chuckled, followed by his father.

"That's quite the young man you have there Carver," Paul said.

"He certainly pays attention, even when you don't think he is."

"If you'll excuse me, dad, I'm going to… uh," he was going to say 'check on Portia' but realized he couldn't say that, "make sure Mom has everything she needs."

He nodded to both men as he left. The dull roar of the dining room faded behind him as he headed upstairs to his room. Empty. One of the waiters walked by him and he caught a scent of fear on the man. He turned to follow when Monique came up behind him.

"Kirk, is everything okay?"

"Yes, I was just… uh," his face blushed.

She smiled. "I left her in the guest quarters; I'm sure she wouldn't mind you stopping by."

Kirk kissed her offered cheek before taking the steps down two at a time, the smell of fear on the caterer forgotten. He restrained himself from running, tension building in him with each step. What would he say to her? How could he explain the way he felt? Technically, he had only been a man for a few days, but his heart burst with love for her. With each step closer to the guest quarters, he felt that his chest would explode. At the top of the stairs her door opened. She was leaving for something. Or someone. His heart fell.

She wore her hair up, with little blonde trails falling down the side of her face. Her feet were all that was visible under a white robe she swaddled herself in.

"Kirk," she squeaked, "what are you doing here?"

He struggled for words; how could he explain his presence? Did he even know?

"Uhm, I wanted to see you," he said lamely, his face heated with each word, "but if you're seeing someone else I'll go." He didn't wait for an answer, instead turning toward the stairs letting each footfall land like a drum at a funeral.

A hand pulled at his shoulder, he shrugged it off, anger building in him.

"Kirk, you idiot, I was coming to see you," she said behind him.

He spun around. "Really? You like me?" he asked, hating the way he sounded so eager.

"Come into my room and I'll show you," she said as she turned. She let the robe fall open and he caught a glimpse of her creamy white skin underneath it.

Heat rolled out of the room as he entered. The guest rooms were not huge, but large enough for a double bed, dresser, and a stand with a flat screen TV. Portia twirled to face him, letting the robe slide off her shoulders as she did so. Each inch revealed creamy white skin; it slipped over her melon sized breasts, resting for a moment on her nipples before falling to the floor.

Kirk gulped, unable to take his eyes off of her gorgeous body.

"Are you going to stand there, or do something about it?"

He pulled off his shirt revealing his hard six-pack and taut muscles that his oversized clothes hid.

"Wow," she whispered. He pulled her close to him; she smelled of jasmine and vanilla. He buried his face in her neck, his tongue exploring the curve to her ear. She gasped as his hands roamed down to her ass. She moaned as he traced her jaw to her lips and kissed her deeply. Their hot tongues mingled and fought as they explored each other's mouths. He walked with her to the wall, never leaving her mouth with his. Bracing her, he lifted her up and she hooked her ankles behind his back. He could feel his erection pressing against her sensitive areas through his pants.

"Is this what you want?" he asked quietly.

"Yes, oh my god, yes, from the moment I saw you, something inside of me snapped. I want to spend my life with you, make babies for you, please, oh god, fuck me," she pleaded.

Kirk's momentary astonishment faded fast as she pushed her pelvis forward. Wolves didn't suffer from lack of action, and they mated for life. He growled as their kissing resumed. His hands roamed up to her tits, squeezing and massaging her nipples. She moaned as his pants slid down revealing his massive cock.

"Will I be one of you?"

"If we have a child, then yes, I can turn you if you want."

He couldn't contain himself anymore. He heaved her over to the bed, pouncing on top of her.

*

Cold water pounded down over Monique's naked body, partially cleansing the lust she felt when she thought of Paul. A new wave of guilt, followed by need, flowed through her. She loved Carver, of that there was no doubt. Since she loved him, she couldn't act on this. Couldn't let some other man, no matter how powerful his draw, pull her from Carver. Without realizing, she slipped her fingers between her legs; the instant satisfaction elicited a moan from her lips.

Fuck, even under a cold shower I'm as hot as an oven.

She turned the water off. If it wasn't going to help there wasn't any need to be in it. The cotton robe hung where she left it. This late in the fall, the rooms were cool and only needed heating at night. Letting the robe hang open, she sat at her desk. Digging around for a minute, she found a pen and paper and started writing. She worked on the first paragraph for a moment before crumpling it up and throwing it in the wastebasket. She needed to leave, at least for a couple of days. Not without explaining things to Carver, though. He could smell her attraction to Paul, as could the senator. That's why she needed to go.

A soft knock on her door interrupted her. The wastebasket sat half full of crumpled paper; this was getting her nowhere.

"One sec," she muttered, frustrated. The door opened to reveal Paul. His presence hit her like a hammer. The soft smell of cologne and musk, his hard blue eyes, the curve of his jaw. She whimpered. Her mind caved and a single tear dropped down her right cheek. She wouldn't be able to resist him, not this close.

He opened his mouth, as if to speak, but instead stepped inside the room. She felt herself move back to let him in. She fought it, but a haze of indecision rolled over her mind. Clouded by the burning desire to feel his touch, to have him take her.

He walked into her room, looked around, taking in the bed, the sparse decorations, the bare walls. The only thing that would tell anyone that the room belonged to her was a photo of two people, holding a little girl. She flinched when he reached out to her. The wolf behind his face grinned—she could feel her attraction to him.

"Please," she whispered as he moved closer to her, "I don't want this." He paused for a moment. Her head felt like a jumbled mass of ideas, of needs, she wanted to be more than her base lusts, but around him that seemed impossible.

"We're wolves Monique, we take what we want, and we dominate. I don't expect you to understand that, but Carver does, he knows you're mine now. It's as simple as that." He smiled as he spoke.

Monique tapped into her well of rage, fists clenched.

"I'm not something you can own, Paul," she said. "I'm not a mindless slave of Carver's; this is as much my home as it's his." Her accent came out in her voice making her words have an over-pronounced quality. Despite her feelings, they were physical, not mental; the only thing she felt for Paul was a physical need to be fucked by him. When she thought of love, of compassion, of all the things that made her heart beat, it was Carver's face.

"We don't control these things Monique, they control us. It's what makes us different, it's what allows to produce genetically superior offspring. When Portia finds a wolf that makes her feel this way, it will be her duty to have children with him, just like it's yours to bear mine." He reached out and grasped the edge of her robe. It slid off her body slowly, the fuzzy material scraping her skin sending little bolts of electricity through her. Goosebumps popped up all over her. He smiled as she squirmed, standing naked in front of him.

She closed her eyes, not wanting to be looked at, but unable to resist. An image flashed in her mind; she could see Portia, in a robe like the one that now lay at her feet. The robe fell to the floor and strong hands pulled her into an embrace.

"I think you're going to have to test that theory," Monique said through deep breaths.

"What?"

"She found that wolf; they're together right now."

"That's not possible, I made sure of it." Paul shook his head, he was right in front of her now. His hands glided up her arms, her body mere inches away from him. Somehow he'd taken his shirt off. His muscles rippled with excitement. Fingers gently guided her jaw up, his lips brushed against her.

In her mind she fought, screamed, railed against this. He was right though, the wolves did things differently and there was only so much she could do to stop it but… Pain shot through her. She heaved Paul away to slam in the wall opposite. Her legs gave out and she slumped to the floor.

"Monique, what's wrong?"

She writhed on the floor for a moment, limbs twitching as if she were electrocuted. Spittle flew from her mouth and she screamed. Then it was gone. She blinked a few times to clear her head.

Kirk!

Something hurt him. Monique heaved herself up, her own muscles rippling with the urge to shift. She had to get outside first—none of her forms were that suited for indoors. She stalked out with Paul following close behind her, barraging her with questions she couldn't hear. Her sole focus was to find Kirk.

The two of them turned at the end of the hall and ran straight into Carver. He smiled in confusion when he caught sight of her naked body. The frown and hurt that followed when Paul appeared without his shirt right behind her burned in her brain. She didn't have time for it now.

"What's going on?" he said barely above a whisper, his voice thick with emotion.

"Kirk," was all she could say, her whole being focused on finding him. There was really only one place he could be. The window on the stairs would do. She threw the window open, and leapt. Paul yelled after her, but his voice was lost in the scream of the hawk.

She cut sharp and up. Being on the opposite side of the building, she needed to get around and over it fast. Once above, she spied two of the senator's SUVs parked with their engines running. The agents carried two sleeping forms into the front one.

Her inner-beast roared as they made off with Kirk and Portia. She folded her wings in and dove to the ground in the blink of an eye. Three agents stood on guard behind the lead SUV as it drove off.

Monique shifted as she touched the ground, her hawk becoming a polar bear. They screamed. The small, black automatic weapons lit up the night. Stinging pain shot up and down her as the sprayed bullets into her skin. The tail lights of the first SUV rapidly disappeared down the road. She needed to hurry. With a roar, she swiped at the closest one. Too stunned to move, he took it in the chest. His body crumpled to the ground. The next one screamed as she crushed his arm with her massive jaws. The last one tried to get in the vehicle. She dragged him out by his ankles. He turned and fired his pistol into her at point blank range.

She tossed his broken body aside with a jerk of her head. The lights were gone now, the road was dark. The bear's job was done. She shifted into her leopard.

"Monique, wait!" Carver yelled behind her. She had no time though. As fast as she was as a hawk, she couldn't see that well at night. Only the leopard could see well enough, and run fast enough to keep up. The vehicles were limited in speed by the curvy road, but that was only true for the first few miles. Once they hit pavement—Kirk was gone. Her sharp howl split the night as she charged down the road.

The cold air whipped by her face. Her paws gripped the dirt road until it curved, then she leaped into the bush to rush down the switchback and gain distance. Her ears picked up the sound of a heavy vehicle. They ran with their headlights off as they cruised down the dirt road. Claws sunk into the dirt inches behind the truck; she hadn't been fast enough. Without missing a beat, she heaved her legs into motion. The road continued to switch back for another half mile—she had one more chance to get them. Over a dead log and she was back in the forest, darting under trees and through brush.

The road approached, and this time she was well ahead of the escaping vehicle. She skidded to a halt in the dirt, coming to rest in the middle of the road. The engine revved up as the driver spied her in the middle of the road. He intended to hit her.

Monique put her shoulder forward and shifted into the bear. The brakes were too late. Two tons of truck hit one ton of bear. Metal collapsed, glass shattered, bone broke, as the truck and Monique collided. Bear and metal rolled into the trees in a horrific crash of flesh and metal.

The world stopped spinning and she felt her strength flee. Her body shifted back into human, broken, bleeding, and bruised. She could see the stars from where she lay on her back. *Carver… I'm sorry.* Blackness took her.

CHAPTER 16

Warmth rolled over her where she lay. Her eyes fluttered open, taking in the stars. She took a deep breath as the memory of the impact washed over her. The speeding truck slammed into her polar bear, sending both over the cliff. Monique winced in agony as she pulled herself up. Ribs ground against each other, blasting her with pain that threatened to black her out. She fell back on the ground.

She turned her head experimentally. To her right, the SUV lay upside down, its front end caved in. The twisted metal was barely recognizable as a vehicle. They'd rolled down the cliff for three hundred feet before coming to rest at the lip of the gorge. She spread her hands out; the lip of the gorge was only a few feet to her right.

Okay, move carefully, get to the SUV, get Kirk out.

The exposed bottom of the car burned. Monique felt the heat from the flames warming her skin, now that she could see it. The orange fire lit up the immediate area. She grunted as one of her ribs slipped back into place. The bones knitted together as her body did its best to heal her from the massive trauma the accident caused. Not to mention the gunshots that got through her tough skin. Bears were tough, but not bulletproof. The adrenaline that surged through her when Kirk was in trouble was long gone. Now everything hurt.

Holding her ribs with one hand, she made her way to the SUV. Unable to stand, she crawled as best she could. The passenger side faced her. The driver's body was a mess of blood and tissue. No one was in the passenger seat. The back window must have been bulletproof since it wasn't shattered so much as bent. She spun on her back and kicked it with her feet. The tough glass bounced a few times before finally caving in. Her feet came away bloody from cuts and scrapes.

"Kirk!" she screamed as she poked her head inside.

No one sat in the back. Both bench seats were empty with no sign of him. The flames roared to new life, the heat forcing Monique back. The car would act as a beacon to the rescue party, but it would take them hours to get down here. She didn't have that kind of time to wait—she needed to find them now.

The moon stood considerably higher in the sky than when she first saw it. She figured she'd been out for roughly thirty minutes, maybe an hour. That gave the people who had Kirk a big head start.

The SUV burned fiercely as she circled it, she had to keep her distance because of the heat, but at least it provided plenty of light. On the opposite side, she spied drag marks in the ground. She knelt down to examine them. Two legs dragged from the SUV. The light from the fire extended a hundred feet, she could see the marks continued on, but after that it was too dark to see.

With one hand on her ribs to ease the ache, she took a tentative step. Her feet hurt with each step. The light behind her faded as she hobbled further away from the wreck. Scrub brush and loose gravel made up most of the bank the road rested on. It took a year and a lot of money to have it carved into the side of the mountain. Now Monique wished it wasn't here at all. The tracks continued parallel to the road for hundreds of feet. The dragging stopped and turned into the footprints of two people walking. An hour passed as she limped along before her ribs healed, followed by her feet. By the time she reached the road, her body felt good as new, though her stomach growled with hunger from all the calories she expended to get there.

She knelt down on the dirt road to get a better look at the tracks. The compact surface was considerably harder to scuff, so seeing the tracks in the moonlight was nearly impossible. They were certainly heading uphill, not down like she would think. Why up? If they were trying to get away, then going down made sense. If they were meeting someone, then the same. There wasn't anything up the mountain except the resort and scattered hunting lodges.

Monique shrugged, it made no difference. With her wounds healed, she felt good enough to shift. The moonless night meant she was better off being a cat than a hawk. With a growl, she changed into her snow leopard. Padded feet made less noise than a whisper. Her sensitive nose picked up Kirk's scent, along with Portia, and two others she didn't recognize. Though one seemed vaguely familiar.

The trail wound up the mountain side, avoiding the resort by heading east. After half an hour, it left the road and went into the woods. *Something's not right here.* Monique couldn't think of a single reason why they would go into the woods.

They had to know what the pack was capable of on the mountain.

*

"Help me!" Kirk screamed. He kicked the door with both feet. Every muscle in his was body energized from adrenaline. The vinyl on the inside of the door tore away as he kicked it. Portia lay unconscious next to him; he could hear her breathing at least. He tried not to look at the driver. The front of the SUV was partially collapsed, the poor man had been crushed under it. He kicked again, the metal bent with a screech.

Agent Nah collected her wits and pushed with him. The door tore open and he was free. He scrambled back in to pull Portia out. Her seatbelt came undone easily enough. He put his arms under her shoulders to drag her out. As he backed out of the SUV, he felt the cold metal of a gun press against his spine.

"I know exactly what you are. You can't dodge this, and she certainly can't. Behave and she lives, misbehave and I swear I will kill her before you can blink. Understand?"

Genuine fear pumped through his veins. He'd never felt such overwhelming agony before. He looked down at her unconscious, heart-shaped face and his heart bled for her. In that moment, he realized he would do anything to keep her safe.

"Yes, just don't hurt her," he said, his voice thick with emotion. The gun vanished from his back and the agent helped him pull her out. They dragged her a few feet from the SUV. A small fire burst to life in the under carriage. In the growing light, Kirk caught a glimpse of a bare foot through the opposite window. The smooth black skin could only be Monique. He hadn't seen what caused the accident, but the way the driver screamed, he could only imagine that Monique had scared the crap out of him. He longed to run to her, to make sure she was okay, but he had to have faith in her. To trust that she would be all right. He couldn't have that same trust that Portia would be. If he left her alone, there was no telling what the agent would do to her.

"Listen, you have me. Leave her here for the others to find." He reasoned he could trade himself for her. After all, he was important. This wasn't the first time someone tried to kidnap him.

"What? Why would I want you?" Nah's gun was out in a flash, barrel pointed at his chest.

"Because I—" what could he tell her? He was some sort of chosen one? No, that wouldn't work.

"My father's rich," he said lamely.

"So is hers, but this isn't about money. Pick her up; we need to go and I need you to carry her."

Kirk lifted her gently; she mumbled as he put one arm over his shoulders and then lifted her legs. She didn't weigh much to him, though he was certainly stronger than the average seventeen-year-old. Despite the circumstances, it felt right to be holding Portia. When they came for them in her room, she hadn't time to put anything on. She wore the only thing she could, a flimsy nightgown that revealed almost everything. He blushed as he looked down at her. To him, she was the most beautiful thing he could imagine.

For someone kidnapping their boss' daughter, and having it go horribly wrong, Agent Nah seemed calm. She also seemed to know exactly where they were going. She led them up to the road, then east, back the way they came.

"Nah," a voice called out from the darkness. The agent spun, weapon out in a blink of an eye. An attractive woman, dressed in a suit similar to Nah's, came out of the brush. Kirk recognized her as one of the caterers. *What is going on?*

"I thought you didn't make it," she said to her cohort. They hugged and looked at him holding Portia.

"Is she still alive?" the newcomer asked.

"He'd be crying like an infant if she wasn't. Come on, we don't have much time."

The road curved up the mountain, but they took off into the woods, staying the course of heading east.

"She needs medical help, she's not like us." Kirk took a chance that there was more to these two than met the eye.

Nah looked back at him, her hand tightening around her pistol. "You don't know what 'we' are, boy. But we know what you are." She waved to her partner. "Check her out."

Kirk put her down as gently as he could, resting her head on his shirt. As he stood back waiting, giving her plenty of room, he took a moment to survey the odds. If they knew he was a wolf, then they knew he was fast. Maybe they were, too, though he should have been able to smell it this close.

Gingerly he leaned against a tree, twisting right to left to make sure his sweat wiped off on the bark. If anyone was following—and he was sure they were—this would help.

"She's got a possible concussion, a few broken ribs, and a lot of bruises; she won't make it to the rendezvous point," her nameless partner announced.

"Shit! Well, we can't give up, and we can't take her to the resort. What does that leave us?" Nah said.

"We maintain a hunting cabin a few hours hike up the mountain. It has medical supplies and a radio. You could call whoever you're meeting to pick you up there," Kirk offered, trying to sound reasonable. The two kidnappers looked at each other for a moment.

"She should make it there," the nameless one said.

"Pick her up, but if she dies," Nah racked the slide on her pistol, a silver colored bullet ejected from the port. She caught it in mid-air, "so do you."

Kirk swallowed with a loud gulp.

THE FINAL CHAPTER

"How long till your people get here, Paul?"

Paul snarled as he put the cell phone down. "This *was* my people, or at least some of them. The agency has people on the way by helicopter, two hours to touchdown."

"I can have the pack out there and searching now, almost thirty of us. This is our mountain, we could find her and have her back before your backup arrives." Carver was already moving to the door to give the order when Paul put a hand on his shoulder.

"No. It's a nice offer, but your people aren't prepared to deal with this, and we don't need good intentioned amateurs out there endangering my daughter."

Carver bristled, but kept control at the slight.

"Okay, we'll play it your way… for now."

Paul nodded. "God, Carver, I'm sorry, they have your son too. I'm being insensitive."

It hadn't occurred to Carver to be concerned about either Kirk or Monique… until that moment. Even now, thinking of the two of them out there, he smiled.

"What so funny?"

"You asked me if I believed in Kirk, and I told you I didn't know. But what I do believe in is Monique. If they have her, or she's chasing after them…" He whistled. "Then they're in more trouble than they can possibly know. How about I call down for some food, and I'll tell you a little story about her."

Paul nodded. Carver picked up the phone and ordered enough food to last the night.

*

The wind whistled through the trees sending a cold chill down his spine. If he were cold, then he knew Portia had to be freezing. Her fingers had a tinge of blue on them, as did her lips. The cabin was hours away. She didn't have that kind of time.

"Agent Nah, right? She's not going to make it to the cabin, we need to find a place to hole up and light a fire. She's going to freeze to death."

The two kidnappers looked at each other, then around the woods. The night was long and cold. There wasn't anywhere for them to go, or for him to run to. And if he did run, he would be leaving her, and he wouldn't do that.

"Do the math, if she dies from hypothermia or from a concussion, she's still dead."

"Take your clothes off and put them on her—we didn't plan to walk out of here."

While he stripped, the other woman rounded up a few sticks, enough to make a small fire. They positioned it behind an upturned tree, enough to block the light.

Damn, they know what they're doing. He vaguely hoped the fire would draw attention, but unless someone came very close, they wouldn't see it. The campfire lit with a few strikes. She kept it small, enough to produce heat with minimal light and smoke. Kirk sat cross-legged in front of it with Portia in his lap and as much of him around her as he could manage. His body temperature ran a few degrees hotter than a normal human.

Nah stood guard on them while her assistant disappeared into the dark.

"What's your plan here Nah? Kidnap Portia for money?" What Kirk couldn't figure out was that they knew about the wolves, so why her instead of him?

"This isn't about money. It's a message. Your kind has pushed us to this. We were few in number to begin with, then you came, pushing us further and further into the woods. You've left us with no choice."

Kirk opened his mouth, but was interrupted by the other person's return.

"We need to move—something is following us."

"Is she ready?" Nah asked.

Her skin had returned to its normal color and her cheeks were flush, Kirk's warmth was keeping her alive. They stayed to either side of him, keeping him flanked. Even if he moved fast enough to take one of them down, the other would get Portia. He had no good options but to go along and hope it played out in a way he could save her.

The terrain didn't get any easier as they climbed the mountain. The dark sky turned gray. And before long, pink. The sun was sneaking up on them, and once it hit the side of the mountain, Kirk would have a better chance at escaping. The cold morning left a chill on him, but at least his warmth kept Portia alive.

"You're shifters aren't you, but not wolves?" he said, things clicking together in his head. *Why hadn't I noticed it before?*

They glanced at each other, Nah giving an almost imperceptible nod.

"You're smart. Yes, we're shifters. Now, come on. Whoever is following us isn't far behind."

Portia stirred. Her hand drifted up to her head.

"Ow," she muttered. Kirk smiled, he kissed her head.

"How you feeling?" he said as they started their hike again.

"Like I got hit by a truck. What happened?"

He dropped his voice to a whisper, "Monique happened."

Her eyebrow quirked up, she tried to move her head. She moaned aloud.

"You've got a concussion, and some broken ribs, we're trying to get you to some medicine right now."

"I'm cold." She shivered, leaning her head against his chest. He smiled, despite the situation, he enjoyed the proximity they shared.

"Why are you naked?" she muttered.

"To keep you warm. Try to stay awake, okay?"

"So tired," she said, her eyes drifting shut.

He jostled her until her blue eyes opened again.

"Stay awake. Tell me about your home?"

"There's a strawberry bush in our backyard, I love the way it smells in the spring…" Kirk did his best to keep her talking. All the while his mind was working on a plan. Whatever they were up to, they wanted Portia, and if it wasn't for money… they wanted to turn her. Whatever they were, there was only one way to turn a woman. And he didn't like this at all. She was his. Their nature demanded it. If another shifter was going to steal her from him, they were going to have a hell of a fight on their hands.

The old growth forest loomed ahead of them. While they seemed to have an idea of where they were going, he knew these lands like the back of his hand. His only liability was Portia. She could barely stay awake, let alone run. He couldn't carry her as a wolf either.

"I need a rest, I can't keep carrying her without any food or water," he said plainly. It was the truth. Even with his strength and endurance, he would need to eat at some point.

"Over there." Nah pointed at a fallen log. Her partner held back, hand on her pistol.

The wind shifted suddenly. A familiar scent wafted past Kirk's nose. He smiled; she would be there soon.

"Wake up Portia, hang in there honey." He kissed her head. The two women looked on, a worried expression clouding their faces.

"Have you two…?" Nah asked.

Kirk hesitated; he wanted to lie, but he simply wasn't good at it. And if they were shifters, they would know.

"What if we have?"

Nah fell on him in a blink. Her hand wrapped around his neck, jerking him away from Portia with a strength he couldn't believe. She held him up against a tree with one hand, her breathing coming in ragged clumps.

"What are you?" he managed as she squeezed his throat shut.

"You think you *wolves* are all there is in the forest? You better not have deflowered her, or your death will be painful and slow, along with her."

Kirk managed to shake his head. The truth was they were interrupted before they did much more than make out.

The tree next to her partner shook. Nah screamed as massive white paws reached out and tore her away from Kirk.

*

Kirk's legs throbbed. The burning was long gone, now each leg felt like a numb block as they fell with each step. Portia's eyes opened. Her pupils widened as she saw the sky above.

"How long have I been out?"

"Hours," he huffed.

He leaned against a tree, not sure if he could take another step. She slid out of his grip, taking her own feet with wobbling legs.

"Good god, Kirk, how far have you carried me?" she looked down the mountain, from this height she could see the valley far below. The morning mist surrounding the trees and rivers obscured the road and the resort.

"Maybe three miles, and about seven thousand feet. We're heading for the winter cabin. You looked like you needed first aid and it was the only place I could think of that might have it. They agreed and we've been on the move since last night. But that's all changed now."

In the morning light, Portia looked as beautiful as ever to him. The sun caught her golden hair and shone through it, sending rays of light behind her.

"Where are they?"

"Close, but the cabin is right up there. And it will have a radio, and guns, maybe we can hold out long enough…"

She reached out and took his hand. Her cold fingers sliding between his.

"I think I love you," she said, the shock of her own words clearly written on her face.

"My father always spoke of this, a love that burns in our breasts from the moment we lay eyes on the right person. I… knew that was what it was the moment I smelled you. I want to spend the rest of my life with you."

She nodded, took his face in her hands, and kissed him on the lips. He encircled her with his arms, drawing her close. Their lips spread open slowly, taking a moment to explore each other. Warmth flooded them both. Kirk sighed internally. This is where he wanted to be, forever and ever.

When they finally broke their embrace, the sun had moved noticeably.

"What do they want? Money?" she asked looking down the mountain hoping to catch a glimpse of the people chasing them. Kirk stood tentatively, not sure if his legs would support him. When they did, he took a step toward the cabin.

"We should go," he said without looking at her.

"Kirk, what do they want with me?"

He just professed his love for her, he didn't want the next thing he told her to be quite so horrific. Ultimately, she had the right to know. He sighed.

"They're werebears… I guess, and they have some sort of beef with your dad," he said without looking at her.

"I didn't know there was such a thing… but I guess if werewolves are possible," she let it hang a moment. "They want to kidnap me for leverage? Makes sense, my dad has a lot of pull with the Alphas."

He took her hand as they started the trek to the cabin. There was more, of course.

"They wanted to give you to their leader, who would turn you into one of them," he said quickly. He wasn't sure of all the specifics himself.

"If they're anything like wolves that means… Oh," she said quietly. "Let's hurry."

The two moved as fast as Kirks tired legs would carry them. His muscles were rested enough that they were back to burning with each step. The rocky ground made it difficult to go very far without slipping and falling. After what felt like an hour, they reached the door of the cabin.

"What took you so long?" Monique asked from behind the recently-cut wood pile. Somewhere she found clothes and a very large rifle.

"She woke up, and I needed a rest. How far behind are they?"

"Not far. I called your dad, they should be here soon," she said as she broke cover to usher them inside. Johan waited for them with two cups of hot cocoa. Along with eggs and thick strips of bacon.

"Seriously?" Kirk asked. The cocoa went down smooth and he immediately felt better.

"You're going to need your strength for what's next," she said with a sly smile.

Portia went to the table, the food laid out looked too appetizing for her not to eat.

"What's the plan and do I get a gun?" Kirk asked.

Monique shook her head. "There's just the one. I would rather have a bow, but I know how to use it. Do you love her?"

Monique's question caught him off guard. He glanced over to Portia's slim form as she ate her food. His heart swelled with desire when he looked at her. She stopped eating to look at him as if she knew. The warm smile that spread across her face reflected his own feelings.

"Yeah, I do."

"Good, then get some food, you're going to need your strength." Monique didn't answer any of his other questions. He resigned himself to doing as he asked. She left the room, and a minute later he heard the shower come on.

"What's going on?" Portia asked.

"Your guess is as good as mine," he said with a shrug.

Johan walked through the room from the small closet with towels in one hand and soap in the other. Kirk focused on eating. A blush started at his feet and spread to his face as he put together what their plan was.

Before Portia could ask him what was going on, Monique came out to get her. She went with her, giving Kirk a sideways look.

Kirk went to the window after he finished eating. If the bears got here before his dad, there wouldn't be enough time to do anything, let alone what Monique had planned.

*

Carver paused at the top of the ridge. His sensitive nose sniffed the air. *Close.* Whoever was after Kirk and Portia wasn't alone. And they were adept at hiding their scent. But not as good as Carver was at finding it. Twenty-one wolves spread out behind him as he turned, including Paul's tawny wolf. His whole pack wasn't there, but close enough. Each one would be willing to die for him, and they made sure he knew it.

The scent went up the mountain after heading east for more than an hour. Once they made the turn uphill, Carver figured out where they were heading. The cabin. It had to be Kirk's idea. Whether he knew Johan was there or not, the kid would have backup. After Monique's call for help, they tried to call her back, but the radio's receiver must be on the fritz. Part of why he sent Johan up there in the first place. A nudge from his side caught his attention.

It will be okay. The tawny wolf seemed to tell him.

Carver growled. *Damn right.* The pack was riled up. No one threatened an entire pack without facing their wrath. Even without pack magic there would be hell to pay, with it, each one of them felt the anger and outrage of their alpha.

The pack charged on, wolf paws dug into the ground with each step, propelling them closer to the top of the mountain.

*

Monique let out the breath she'd been holding. The first one came into her sights five hundred yards away. Its shaggy brown coat glistened in the sun. She wanted to pull the trigger, but if they knew she had a rifle, they may change their plans. And she wanted them as close as possible. They needed to hear it.

"They're here—you'd better change," she said to Johan.

He nodded. Already naked, he didn't have to take his clothes off. His body shivered as his skin morphed from pink to brown then to fur. He fell over on all fours with a grunt that turned into a growl.

More and more bears emerged from the tree line. She counted five before *he* came out. He had to be the leader. The other bears were smaller, more round—he was massive, shoulders like boulders as he stomped over the ground. She looked down at the rifle, it was small compared to him.

The door to the bedroom creaked open, Kirk's face in the opening.

"Monique," he pleaded.

"It's the only way. He's here for one thing, and he can't have it."

"How do you know it works?"

She smiled. "Trust me, it works. Now get in there, and I'd better hear some activity."

He blushed and shut the door. Monique never figured she would be encouraging a young couple to fuck. If they didn't though, the bear would take her and rape her. And that wouldn't be pleasant at all. It's not like this wasn't what they were going to do the night they were taken. She just needed them to commit. It wouldn't hurt if Portia was impregnated to boot. It would seal an alliance between Paul and Carver, and help them deal with their other problems. Even now, with a shaggy death facing them, the thought of those two men sent a shiver up her spine.

The leader, flanked by his bears, stopped a hundred yards from the cabin. He reared up on his hind legs, thick brown hair vanished and a man stood there. His manhood was undeniable. Thick hair covered his torso, along with long brown hair that flowed past his shoulders.

"Send out the girl," he roared.

"If all you want is a girl, I'm sure we can arrange something," Monique yelled back from the window.

He smiled. "I give you full marks for bravery, but don't be stupid. You can't hope to stop us, wolf," he growled.

Monique held her hand out to Johan to heel. The last thing she needed was for him to charge out and get himself killed. She cocked her head toward the bedroom and listened. A soft moan drifted across the room. *Good, they've started.*

Now she needed Carver to get here before they killed her. That would be perfect. She stepped out of the cabin. The rifle was leaning against the inside of the door, all she would have to do was reach in and she would have it.

"What's your name?" he asked. She noticed he moved forward as he spoke.

"Monique," she replied. Her eyes flickered to the bears on either side closing in around the cabin.

"Surely your life, and the life of the other two wolves in there, isn't worth one worthless girl."

"I like her," Monique said flatly. "That makes her worth something."

She heard a grunt from the bedroom, Portia's voice carried to her, "Oh god, fuck me!"

She smiled. *Any second now.*

"Nevertheless, she's mine. Her father must learn the error of his ways." He wasn't more than thirty feet away now. Bears had exceptional hearing, almost as good as a wolf could smell. If that held true for him, he would hear any second.

"Oh god, I'm cumming," Portia screamed form behind the door.

"Oops… too late shaggy, sounds like she's taken."

Rage flooded his features. He transformed from man to bear in the breadth of a step. Monique hauled the rifle up, slammed the stock into her shoulder, brought the barrel on target, and fired. The weapon's massive round kicked her like a mule. The bullet ripped through the bear, blood and sinew splattering the ground behind him.

The other bears roared and charged. Monique held her ground. Exhausted from lack of sleep, and over taxed from her own shifting, she had to face them as a woman. She popped the breach open and dropped another massive shell in. With no time to aim, she fired from the hip. The closest bear dropped when it's head exploded.

She flung herself back out of the way as a paw swiped the air where she had been. The cabin floor slammed her back and she kicked the door closed with her feet. Wood splintered as the bear crashed his massive paws into it. Teeth the size of her hand dug into the old frame and ripped bits out.

"Johan, protect Kirk!"

Exhausted as she was, she stood no chance against the bear. "Come on Carver, where are you?!" she hissed.

As if to answer her call, the howl of wolves broke the noise of the furious bear. Johan suddenly charged the door. The bear turned to fight behind it and Johan bit deep into his shoulder. Monique reloaded the rifle. She shattered the window to shoot out. The pack was there. And they brought everyone.

She fired again at the closest bear. It roared from the hit. The bears backed away as Carver and Paul circled the cabin. As many bears as there were, there were too many wolves to fight without losing too much.

The leader backed away from the cabin, leaving a trail of blood. When he got to the treeline, he looked back to Monique before disappearing. Exhaustion flooded over her. It was done. Carver was there, in human form holding her up, then Paul.

"Is she okay?" he asked her. She couldn't help but notice how naked the two men were.

"Yes, but you may not like why," she said.

Kirk and Portia exited the cabin wrapped in a sheet, a spot of blood on it told her that their plan worked. Monique sunk into Carver's chest, unable to stay awake any longer.

*

Monique sighed as she signed the last check for the summer. Winter was upon them now. Snow fell silently outside the window. It always brought a smile to her face. Everyone else feared the snow, feared how it bound them to shelter; for her, she felt like it freed her.

Kirk and Portia were away at her mom's. She had a lot of explaining to do and the couple needed some time to get to know each other before the wedding. They planned it for the spring, hopefully Portia wouldn't be showing by then, it made wedding dress shopping a lot easier.

Everything else was back to normal. Paul's pack and Carver's would be formalizing a new relationship soon. With the marriage of their children, they had no choice but to become allies. That and because of her. She couldn't deny how she felt about Paul. It burned in her every second of the day. And it wouldn't stop until he made her his bitch. At the same time, she loved Carver with all her heart. There had to be a solution, and if the packs were allies, that solution would be easier than not.

She sighed, looking at her bags packed in the corner. It wouldn't be easy on any of them, but they had to make it work. When Paul left, she would be going with him. At least until Christmas, to see if this fever she felt would pass. If it didn't, then she would have to schedule her time between Carver and Paul. Things could be worse; one of them could have really bad breath.

With the last check signed, she grabbed a couple of beers out of the cooler. She stopped to change into her bathing suit, which was nothing more than a thong and a see-through wrap. She didn't feel the need for modesty in her private hot tub.

She stepped outside onto the deck, the hot tub had high walls so that it couldn't be spied on from the other balconies. She climbed the ladder, beers in one hand. When she reached the top she let out a gasp. Paul was there, and behind him, Carver. Neither man wore a suit.

"What are you two doing here?"

"We felt, if you were interested, maybe we could get spend some time together before you left."

Monique lifted an eyebrow as the delicious possibilities presented themselves. She slid into the water. Letting her nipples set just above so the cold air made them hard.

"Consider me interested," she said as she embraced Carver.

THE END

Message From The Author:

Hiii

If you want to check out my other releases including those from my popular "Shifters Surrogates" series then just check out [my Amazon page here!](#)

I hope you enjoyed my book. If you did I would really love if you could give me a rating on the store! :)

Angela x

Get Yourself a FREE Bestselling Paranormal Romance Book!

Join the "**Simply Shifters**" Mailing list today and gain access to an exclusive **FREE** classic Paranormal Shifter Romance book by one of our bestselling authors along with many others more to come. You will also be kept up to date on the best book deals in the future on the hottest new Paranormal Romances. We are the HOME of Paranormal Romance after all!

* Get FREE Shifter Romance Books For Your Kindle & Other Cool giveaways

* Discover Exclusive Deals & Discounts Before Anyone Else!

* Be The FIRST To Know about Hot New Releases From Your Favorite Authors

Click The Link Below To Access Get All This Now!

SimplyShifters.com

Already subscribed? OK, *Turn The Page!*

ALSO BY SIMPLY SHIFTERS....

SIMPLY ALPHA WOLVES
A TEN BOOK WEREWOLF ROMANCE COLLECTION

50% DISCOUNT!!

This unique 10 book package features some of the best selling authors from the world of Paranormal Romance. Well known names such as Amira Rain, Jasmine White, Ellie Valentina and more have collaborated to bring you a **HUGE** dose of sexy Alpha goodness. There will be love, romance, action and adventure alongside some hot mating in each of these 10 amazing books.

1 The Alphas Unwanted Mate – Ellie Valentina
2 The Alpha's Surrogate – Angela Foxxe
3 Legend Of The Highland Wolves– Bonnie Burrows
4 The Next Alpha – Jasmine White
5 Chained To The Alpha – JJ Jones

6 The Alphas Mail Order Mate – Jade White
7 The Wolf's Forbidden Baby – Ellie Valentina
8 The Real Italian Alphas – Bonnie Burrows
9 Fated To The Alpha – Jasmine White
10 The Island Of Alphas – Amira Rain

START READING NOW AT THE BELOW LINK!

Amazon.com >
http://www.amazon.com/gp/product/B0167CVA26

Amazon UK >
http://www.amazon.co.uk/gp/product/B0167CVA26

Amazon Australia >
http://www.amazon.com.au/gp/product/B0167CVA26

Amazon Canada >
http://www.amazon.ca/gp/product/B0167CVA26